BONNIE ENGSTROM

Melanie's Ghosts

The Candy Cane Girls, book 7

By Bonnie Engstrom

ISBN-13: 978-1-946939-91-3
ISBN-10: 1-946939-91-9

ABOUT THE CANDY CANES

Ten years ago six high school freshmen in Newport Beach, California formed a swim team that became legendary. They won the state relay swim championship four years in a row. In addition to their skill and devotion to daily practicing, they prayed together and vowed to be sisters forever. Another thing that set them apart was they chose their own swimsuits making them a team within a larger team. They chose red and white diagonally striped swim suits. Thus, became known as the Candy Canes. They always will be.

Dear Reader ~

I hope you will enjoy this series that tells the stories of women who are what I call super friends ~ friends who committed as teenagers to prayer and loyalty bound by a moniker. The Candy Cane Girls are a unique group of sister friends. I hope their stories will inspire other young women. They are Sisters of Promise, promises they made when young and promises they've kept for generations.

I am hoping to start an inspiration, a situation or a way to encourage young women, especially teen girls, to write their own stories. I have three teenage granddaughters who are bright and talented but as far as I know do not record their thoughts and experiences. I also pray for other teen girls of friends. It troubles me they are not writing about their lives and experiences. Please join me in praying for an upcoming of young women writers.

As you read through this series, and I hope you will, please note how each book tells a story about individual women, how each struggle with a personal situation and overcomes it. Some of the circumstances they encounter are destined by faith and fate; but all require belief and commitment to each other and to the faith of each. I hope you will read every story to see how Cindy deals with her new love's health issues, and Candy takes her fears into action, and Connie . . . well she has a problem that she overcomes with the help of sweet Jake, her 'problems solving' dog. Jake will appear in many following books. He was my running companion for many years – the dearest dog. But Lola and Happy Arthur are shining woofers in their own stories.

But wait until you get to Natalie and Melanie! They hold the keys to lasting friendship. Their stories are almost legendary.

All stories in the series can be read individually, but you will enjoy them more and understand them more if you read them in order.

Noelle, Cindy, Connie, Candy, Natalie, Doreen and especially Melanie will steal your heart.

You will have fun with the different wedding venues. How many weddings have you attended in an historical place, or in a hospital lobby or a gym? Maybe these will be your first and most memorable.

You will do me a great favor if you enjoyed this series and write a quick, honest review on Amazon or Goodreads. Just a few words mean a lot and encourage others to read it.

Thank you. If you would like to be connected to me for comments and conversation please sign up for my newsletter at www.bonnieengstrom.com and learn about my writing history. You can email me at bengstrom@hotmail.com. Please put SERIES <in caps) in the subject line. I would love to chat with you.

Special BONUS! The Candy Cane Series is ideal for group discussion, especially for book clubs. I have a special offer for book clubs for all of my books. If you are interested please email me at bengstrom@hotmail.com with CLUB <all caps) in the subject line.

Blessings,
Bonnie

Dedication

Writing the second episode of Melanie's story was a challenge. I couldn't have done it without the help of so many.

My wonderful Beta readers:

- Cheryl Turner, who's read every book of mine. Thank you, Cheryl, for your faithfulness and enjoying my stories.

- Carrie Del Pizzo who asked a lot of questions and found several flaws. Without her dedication this book would not be published.

- Sharon A. Lavy, who also questioned several scenes causing me to go back and rewrite. An important part of writing.

- Liz Thompson who picked up on my re-use of several words. I corrected that, thanks to her.

I am grateful also to the following whose help made the story more genuine.

Ann Allen, dear author friend and Microsoft Word guru who has saved my messes many times. This one included.

Randi Burggraff, a trusted friend and attorney. Not sure if I corrected all the legal stuff she suggested, but "Hey, Randi, it's fiction!" Still, without her guidance and expertise, I would have given up.

David Engstrom, my psychologist husband who checked every comment I made about OCD and said it was "right on." I guess I learned a lot from him in fifty-three years.

Cynthia Hickey, my patient and trusting publisher

at Forget Me Not Romances. Thank you for believing in my stories and The Candy Cane Girls.

Bless you and thanks to you all, for your support and help. **Melanie's Ghosts** is dedicated to you!

Thank you, Jesus, for giving me the courage and patience to write this story and

for leading me to this special Scripture that confirms it all.

Habakkuk 2:3

"For the revelation awaits an appointed time;

it speaks of the end

and will not prove false.

Though it linger, wait for it;

it will certainly come

and will not delay."

Proverbs 19:21 "Many are the plans in a person's heart, but it is the Lord's purpose that prevails."

Prologue

"This is wrong. No sense. Makes no sense."

Melanie embraced his big, strong brown hand between her small white ones. Larry didn't move. He was dead.

~

Melanie sat across the table from attorney Randi. Her fingers were paste white and knuckles blue. Is that what death does? She examined her glittering fingernails; the fancy ones Kay had gifted her with for her marriage to Larry and now insisted she needed again as a boost for the burial. But, their luster was useless. Her life was, too. Her future held no meaning. She was a widow, not a newlywed.

Natalie, her best friend, shifted in her chair. "What is the next step, Randi? Melanie needs somewhere to go in her heart and in her head. She needs to find understanding and peace. What do you suggest?" She looked over at Mel and squeezed her hand, the hand that rested on her special blue skirt, the one she clung to and claimed as her God skirt, the one she wore when she met Larry. What would happen to the skirt now? Would it be folded away in a memory trunk, or maybe destroyed?

Randi, professional attorney as she was, blinked rapidly. Moisture coated her lashes. "I have been trying to decide how to tell you. Not easy."

"Just tell, please. I need to know what to do." Melanie squeezed Natalie's hand tighter.

Randi sighed and pushed a paper toward the two women.

"A list? You are giving me a list?"

"No, I am giving you a suggestion. Hopefully a healing option." She lowered her chin. "Sorry. But I believe this is the one thing that will give you comfort and clarity."

Melanie picked up the typewritten paper, the paper with the single suggestion, and held it in trembling hands. Natalie leaned closer to look. "Oh!" The expletive blew out of her mouth like a gust of dry wind.

Chapter One

Melanie

Newport Beach is a strangely diverse community. Or, should I say town? It claims to be a city, but when you daily run into neighbors in the market or at church or taking a jog, it's really a town.

What is strange about its diversity isn't that it's not all lily white. Not completely. There is the Yu family down the block and Dr. Hawthorne the black doctor who is part of the primary care physician group in Fashion Island. No, what's strange about its diversity isn't ethnicity or color or age. It's the groupings. The family homes, the planned communities as they used to be called; the lavish apartment homes, too pricey for short-term dwellers; the cute condo communities, the ones the empty-nesters downsize to; the raggly, straggly beach bungalows bordering the edge of the bay – summer homes for the financially secure, some who actually live in lavish homes on the hill but want to play on the beach.

I grew up in one of the condos in Eastbluff. Well,

mostly. When my mom's first marriage dissolved, the one after my dad died and she was lonely, we moved from our tract house, the one in the planned community that she and dad had never remodeled. They couldn't afford to. Still, it sold for five times the price they'd paid for it in the seventies. That's how much Newport was sought after for a small plot of land and an old, simple three small bedroom house to be torn down and rebuilt. Crazy.

When Mom and I moved to our cozy condo in The Bluffs I didn't mind. In fact, I loved it. I still attended Vista del Mar High School and could even walk there. I was a slightly above average student with no sights set on a Big Five University. Never athletic, although sports were revered at VDM, I envied the slim, bustless girls who garnered so much attention winning state and regional swim championships. The Candy Canes they were called. For some reason they were allowed to form a team within a team and were also allowed to choose their own swimsuits. Maybe Speedo designed those special red and white striped suits just for them. Maybe because everyone, especially Coach Beckworth, knew they were deemed to be champions. A much-needed accolade for a beach community school way too focused on football.

I will never know if it was fate, God's plan or my stupidity that caused the accident. I had been partying, driving my beloved new red pick-up on Coast Highway. Distracted, and drunk, I ran a red light. That night I met forgiveness. Five girls and a young man surrounded me in a waiting area of Hoag Hospital while Doreen's leg was being operated on, maybe even amputated. The strangest part was those girls and that man, Braydon Lovejoy, prayed for me almost as much as they prayed for Doreen whose life I had almost taken, and certainly damaged.

That's when I knew, that's when I got it.

Faith. Forgiveness. Friendship.

Chapter Two
Natalie

Melanie has become my best friend. I am still close to all the other girls, but something about Melanie tugged at my heart. We became confidants. Maybe because we are the only two of the group who still haven't found lasting love. When we Candy Canes accepted her into our group after she struggled to swim ten laps, she was one of us, forever. Now, I am here beside her. What she is going through is unimaginable. To think I introduced her and Larry blows my mind.

I pick up the paper Randi slid across the table and scan it. The option Randi suggested isn't really a legal one, but one given out of friendship. "Join a grief group." Makes sense to me, but will she? Randi even listed a few websites. I hope and pray Melanie will.

Chapter Three
Melanie

The Funeral

Last week I buried him. I chose a grave instead of an urn. I wanted someplace to visit, kneel down at and place flowers. No one else would honor him this way. I couldn't pass an urn around, even if I ever found relatives. He was a loner, except for me. Besides, I didn't want my little dog Lola sniffing it. Too weird.

All the Candy Canes in the states came. It was a hard decision whether to bury him in California or Arizona. I finally decided Arizona since that's where he was from and where we were married.

Many of the nurses and employees from Honor Health Hospital in Scottsdale came, too. They had been a special part of our wedding in the lobby of Honor Health, even decorated it for the nuptials. I know they loved me, and I believe they loved Larry, too.

I asked Tyler from Hillsong Church where Larry was baptized to say a few words. Hard to imagine how

7

he found those special words. Tyler is only twenty-five. But, he did. He honored Larry and our marriage and gave me comfort.

Chapter Four

Melanie

Scary. I don't want to share what Larry did, don't want to share our love and our brief, almost momentary, marriage. So hard. Natalie says I have to, it will be a release, it will help. I am such a private person. Don't know if I can do it.

I twist the gorgeous blue diamond ring on my finger, click on the grief group website and sign up to attend. I know God put this on my heart, but, *Really, God, am I to expose myself and my beloved this way?*

Thursday night comes, and I halfheartedly go. But, I have a support system. Not only Natalie, but Candy and Noelle, and sweet Doreen. I wonder if anyone will recognize the celebrated model. Probably not since most of the group is wrapped up in their own pain. Still, I am overwhelmed. What love!

We hover behind the semi-circle of folding chairs in the community center, clasp hands and pray.

Natalie gives me a gentle shove, and I walk slowly to the only empty chair, next to a distinguished looking man about my Larry's age. Age being the only shared characteristic. This man is white with a moustache and a very short beard trimmed neatly. His gray hair is certainly premature for his millennial age.

"Sir," the female moderator Annette points to him. "Please start us off."

He removes his glasses and pulls a cleaning wipe of some kind from the pocket of his khakis. Rubbing the lenses slowly, he replaces the wiping thing in his pocket, anchors the tortoise shell frames on the bridge of his nose and begins to speak. Maybe I am paying so much attention to him and his gestures to distract me, hoping to avoid my turn. When he finally speaks his voice is controlled, but low. He lost his wife from months of cancer. I am shocked by his words. He folds his hands on his lap gripping them so tight I notice his knuckles are white.

I am next.

How do I explain? Do I share how we fell instantly in love when he was in a hospital bed? Do I share our beautiful wedding? The gorgeous blue stone I twist on my finger? The deception?

It is my turn to speak but no words come. Natalie reaches over my shoulder and squeezes my right hand, Candy does the same and holds my left, Noelle and Doreen place warm hands on my back. I say a prayer. Finally, I speak and spill it all out. It is a new beginning for me.

Chapter Five
Melanie

The phone call was unexpected. I almost didn't accept it. But, it was from an Arizona number, and I had recently come back from burying Larry there. I picked it up and was shocked.

"Is this Melanie? I am Larry's mother." The person on the other end didn't give me time to respond.

He'd told me his mother left, abandoned him and his dad when he was very young, maybe five or six.

I was confused, stupefied. No words came out. I felt myself landing on the sofa and saying, "What?"

"I said," the unsteady voice repeated, "I am Larry's mother. I think you are his wife."

"Not any more. I am his widow. He is dead." Why did I even respond to this person? "Who are you really?"

"I am his mother," the voice repeated more firmly this time.

"What do you want? He died with nothing, nothing to claim. He was a criminal, died in prison."

"Oh."

"I can't help you if you want money. He didn't have any. He stole it from others." I caught my breath. "So, no money." I shook my head and came to my senses. Who was this woman? How did she know about Larry? Why did I assume she wanted money? Finally I had the presence of mind to ask, "What is your name?"

"Saw the obituary in the paper. I still live in Arizona. Small state. Want to meet you, the girl my Larry loved."

"Why did you leave? When he was a young boy? He longed for you."

"Too much to explain in a phone call. I want to meet you."

"I am back in California, my home."

"So," she said, "I will come there. Need to do this."

How will she get there? Not my problem.

She never gave me her name.

Chapter Six
Melanie

I didn't want this woman to know where I lived. Didn't really trust her. But, if she truly was Larry's mother, although estranged, I need to meet her face to face. We agreed the Starbucks on Pacific Coast Highway in Corona del Mar. I would take a Candy Cane with me. Hopefully, Natalie.

Instead I have Candy. She is the strongest one, twice married to Will who is now recovered from his alcohol problems, a big AA supporter. Candy is so strong because she has been through so much. Noelle is here too but hovers in the background. "Just in case," she says with a small smirk. She is also strong with all she went through with that disgusting man Bruce, my stepfather, who was the high school principal. Noelle likes to be in the background and ready, maybe mentally quoting Shakespeare in her head, English teacher that she is. I am thankful for both of them.

I sit at the small table holding Candy's hand, then look around and my eyes pop. Vivian is here holding Noelle's hand. Vivian the adoptive mom of all the

Candy Canes. What a gift. She will be on top of everything. The woman is amazing. She flew to Scottsdale to take care of Connie during her difficult pregnancy. She interceded for Candy, her own daughter, when Candy was unsure of re-marrying Will. She is the ultimate mom of all the Candy Canes. She is here for me!

Candy grips my hand tighter. "I think she's here."

A tiny dark-skinned woman maybe in her late fifties stands inside the door and squints. She has a strange head of hair. Only a few tufts of black poking up. Dingy mismatched clothes are layered on her short frame. A large, pouchy gray bag hangs from her shoulder. She fiddles with the zipper but doesn't open it. I don't move, just wait. I wonder how she got here, all the way from Arizona. Maybe I'll never know. She fiddles with the zipper again.

Everyone in the coffee shop stops talking. It is very quiet, except for a few slurping sounds. Candy stands up. The woman approaches her. She has a wary look on her face, then speaks hoarsely. "Melanie?"

"No. I'm her friend."

"Oh, that her with the huge blue ring that belongs to me?"

I forgot to turn my ring around to conceal the blue diamond. Stupid. Too late now.

Candy sits down again at our table, and the woman swaggers over, her hand still clutching her bag. She glares at both of us. "Get me some coffee," she demands.

"What would you like?" Candy asks sweetly.

"Venti caramel Frappuccino. Need the calories. Extra whipped cream."

Candy stands up and places the order while the woman just stares at me. Her eyes are penetrating, and I feel beads of sweat on my forehead. I try to pray, but nothing comes.

"So," she finally says. "You're the white girl who seduced my boy."

I don't know where my courage comes from, but I whisper, "You're the mother who abandoned him."

She has placed the gray bag on her lap and her knarled hand keeps rubbing it. What was in it? Should I be scared?

"You don't know the story, girl. There was a reason."

Candy returns with the woman's Venti Frappuccino and sets it down in front of her. She sucks on it hungrily. No thanks or acknowledgement.

Finally, she looks up. "Needed that. Need calories to offset the chemo."

Larry's mother needs chemo? Why did I not know that? Of course, no contact between them for years. Still, it upsets me.

"So," Candy says with a strong voice, "tell us." She fiddles with her latte, then looks up. She never says sorry for the woman's situation. She just asks.

"Been battling cancer for over a year. Bad stuff. Need money. Insurance doesn't pay." She stops for a gasping breath that rattles in her throat.

Candy is strong. She looks the woman in the eyes. "That doesn't answer the question. Why did you leave a child so many years ago?"

The woman looks away and puts her bag on the floor. Her eyes swell with tears. I pray for answers. But they don't come.

Chapter Seven
Melanie

"She wanted your ring."

"Yes. But it's mine now. A gift. I can't give it up. It's all I have left."

"You have wonderful memories, Mel. I know it's hard, but it's time to be realistic."

Candy was tough. She had been through so much herself with Will. Now, she was supporting me. I was grateful for her strength and her wisdom. But, I just wanted to go home and hunker under my down comforter and sleep – forever.

~

The choice wasn't mine, nor Larry's mother's. I was eventually served papers. I probably shouldn't have answered the door, but I had no clue. The server asked my name. I responded. Done deal. The FBI had determined Larry had used the stolen money to purchase my beautiful blue diamond ring. I had to hand it over. I pray the person he stole from will understand how special it is, maybe not sell it for money, but value it. I guess it doesn't matter. It is just a thing. Natalie sent me the description Larry had sent to her about the ring. That will always be on my heart.

Larry's mother disappeared. At least for a while. Then, after a month she came back. I was confused, didn't know what to do. I called a meeting of the Candy Canes.

Chapter Eight
Candy

A mess. Melanie's life is a mess. Confusion. I don't know how to advise her. I am glad we got through the meeting with Larry's mom, but I worry still. The woman is not only weird, but she has an agenda. One I don't trust.

The next morning all we Candy Canes in Newport get together at Nat's Gym. It is an overcast gloomy day, typical Newport with dark clouds hanging over the Pacific. What we Newporters call June gloom, even if it isn't June. We each buzz in, and the secure door opens. Natalie suggested we all do some kind of cardio for even five minutes before we gather to pray. Such a good idea.

I lift eight-pound weights, Noelle does the Stairmaster, my mom Vivian does stretching and cardio, and Nat spots each of us. Melanie must be super nervous because she only does a few squats and twists. None of us can blame her, poor thing. My mom, Vivian, is the only one who has been widowed, but that was years ago. Now she is married to Bill Lord, Senior, who was also widowed when they met. And to think I once had my sights set on him, my now stepdad.

~

Doreen showed up for the prayer part. We were all so glad to see her, especially for her support of Melanie since Mel had caused the accident that caused Doreen to have a deformed leg. Maybe Doreen is the most pious of us all, the one with the deepest faith. Must be, because she led us in prayer. Before we started we got Cindy in Costa Rica and Connie in Scottsdale on Facetime on two of our phones. We were complete. We formed a circle and clasped hands.

"Father God," Doreen bowed her head. "We are so grateful to be able to come to you, and we lift our hearts in praise for Your faithfulness."

Even though my eyes were closed, I sensed all of us nodding in agreement. We do have an awesome and faithful God. Finally, after Doreen asked for wisdom and discernment and protection for Melanie, each of us said a brief petition and a collective "Amen." Melanie was sobbing. She threw her arms around each of us and squeezed my hand so hard I winced. "Now," I whispered, "we wait for His guidance." I hesitated but needed to say it to reassure Mel. "His timing, Mel. Not ours."

I pulled Habakkuk 2:3 up on the Bible app on my phone and read it aloud.

"For the revelation awaits an appointed time;
it speaks of the end
and will not prove false.

Though it linger, wait for it;
it will certainly come
and will not delay."

Melanie nodded. Her face was blotched and wet. "I know," she said. "Waiting is the hardest part. Or, maybe trusting is." She scanned our faces. "I'm not big on patience."

"Maybe," Vivian said, "that's what you need to pray for right now."

BONNIE ENGSTROM

Chapter Nine
Summons

Natalie decided to spend the night at Melanie's for moral support. It was easier than worrying about Lola dog, either leaving her alone or bringing to Nat's with Melanie. Besides, since Nat only had to open the gym in the morning she only needed workout clothes and a pair of PJs. She was planning to sleep until seven, take a quick shower, don her clothes and tennies, then sneak out. The piercing of the doorbell woke her and Lola at six. Lola howled, Nat cursed silently and threw off the covers. Who?

She looked through the peephole, saw a scruffy man dressed in sweats who kept pushing the bell. "Okay, okay. Stop! We hear you. Hang on."

He put his arms to his side, one holding a sheaf of papers. Uh, oh. She thought she knew what he wanted. But, Mel needed to deal with this. She shook her friend awake and explained.

"What does he want? Who is he?"

"I am only guessing, but I think you are being served papers. Court papers."

"For what? I haven't done anything wrong?"

"Doesn't matter. Someone thinks you did. Just by being married to Larry."

"How horrible. Another notch in my aborted marriage."

She opened the door. The man on the other side did look a bit peeved, but when he saw her he looked guilty. His face blanched and his lids dropped. His chin dropped, too. Then, he asked. "Are you Melanie Carson Langston?"

She nodded as he handed her the papers. "Sorry," he said. "Had to do this." He lowered his head and said, "Job." Then he scurried away.

Melanie clutched the papers to her chest. "Why is this happening? I did nothing wrong."

Chapter Ten
Court

"I don't know what to do. It says I have to appear before a judge." Melanie covered her mouth with a hand. "Why? I didn't do anything wrong."

Nat hugged her friend. "Sadly, Larry did. Apparently a lot wrong."

"But, he got baptized. Repented." Melanie's tears stained the papers she still clutched to her breast.

Natalie's hands went to her own breast. "Yes, he has been forgiven by God, but not by man. And apparently not by his mama," she added. She gripped Melanie by the shoulders and turned her friend to face her, eyes locking. "We know he is in heaven, Mel. That is what's important."

Melanie nodded. Tears drying on her cheeks. "Better go get dressed."

~

Because he was arrested in California, she had to go to a court in Orange County. Seemed strange since he stole in Arizona, but the papers dictated it. At least it was convenient.

Melanie and Natalie climbed the two long staircases in the Orange County Courthouse. "Why didn't we take the elevator?"

"Crowded. And we need the exercise to cleanse us to get ready for this."

"Spoken like a true gym owner," Mel quipped.

Forty minutes later Melanie was called to testify. Is that, she wondered, what it is called?

"Yes, I am telling the truth.

"No, I didn't know about Larry taking money from others.

"But, you need to know he became a Christian, even got baptized."

The judge slammed down a gavel. "No more comments."

Melanie fumbled with her ring, twisting it so the stone didn't show. Would she have to give it up? Natalie squeezed her hand and nodded toward a woman sitting in the audience. Larry's mother was there, too. But, another woman sat a few aisles away from her. Was she the woman Larry scammed, the woman whose credit card he used to buy the blue ring?

The hearing, as the court called it, was shorter than she expected. The judge made a decision. Melanie took off her ring and gave it to a court officer. It was over. Done. Hopefully, she was out of Larry's mother's radar. She felt sorry for the woman, but as Natalie said, she was not her responsibility. But, technically, she was Mel's mother-in-law.

~

Melanie shrugged off her jacket and tossed it on her sofa. Lola leaped around her legs just as her phone buzzed. She'd had it on silent because of going to court.

When she saw the screen display New Hope Preschool she knew it was Ms. Dana her boss. She dreaded answering her. Her situation was so embarrassing. She knew Dana cared, had undoubtedly prayed, and wanted to know how the court proceedings went. She finally touched the green button. That's when she started sobbing.

Dana and many of the teachers had come to Larry's funeral, a real commitment of love for them to travel from California to Arizona. Some of the parents came, too. Mostly moms from her class, even a few from other preschool classes. She was very blessed to teach at a Christian school surrounded by believers. Her salary wasn't great, but enough, and the love was great. She agreed to come back on staff. Fortunately, Dana had not filled her lead teacher position permanently. She had a list of substitute teachers, even filled in herself occasionally when one of the teachers was sick or had an ill child. Melanie was excited about next Monday. She had so many ideas for her adorable three-year-olds, and she was anxious to teach again with Nora, even though they'd had some disagreements. She missed them all and needed to get back into a routine and put Larry behind her. She wondered if adorable little Jackson still blew juice bubbles at his classmates.

~

She tugged on her New Hope red tee shirt that said "Christ is the heart of every home" letting it hang over her navy pants. This was going to be a new day, a new beginning. Or, maybe a picked up one. Either way she was excited . . . until her doorbell rang.

What was that woman doing here? How did she find her? She'd peeked out the side glass and almost didn't answer the door hoping Larry's mother would think she had already left for work. *Too honest. Why am I so honest?* She pulled the door open to a woman whose name she still didn't know. A woman with old smeared makeup and a sneer on her face and holding a big gray satchel. The woman turned aside and spit into the bush beside Mel's front walk, then pulled out a cigarette and lighter.

"Not in here. Not on your life. Put that away." Mel wasn't sure why she bothered. She was not going to let this woman inside. The woman's brown face crunched up and she sneered again.

"You gotta see me. I am your mother-in-law. No taking that back."

Melanie prayed, gulped and, with courage, answered the woman. "No. Not any longer. He's dead, so not my husband anymore. No children, no legacy. Goodbye!" She slammed the door hard. *Why, God, is this woman being so persistent? I have nothing to give her. Nothing. She abandoned her child and husband over thirty years ago. Why now?*

She finished dressing and slipped on her tennies, almost a requisite for teaching preschool so not to slip on spilled juice. She pulled her car out of her garage without incident. Until . . . she saw the woman slumped in a heap on the sidewalk in front of her apartment building. Her gray bag was beside her, and she held a hand-printed sign.

"Help me. I am homeless. My family has deserted me."

Melanie almost choked. Bile rose up in her throat. What sort of human being was this? Maybe she was a figment of Mel's imagination.

Chapter Eleven
Melanie

"I can't forget that woman sitting on the stoop of my apartment."

It was the next grief group, and Melanie was sharing. Reluctantly. She was glad she came, even overcoming the stress of her first few days back at teaching. Everyone was so kind and understanding this evening. Especially Robert who sat next to her. He was the one who shared last time about his wife dying. He reached for her hand just before it was her turn to share. His hand was firm and dry, thankfully not sweaty like so many men's. Although there was an antiseptic odor. Still, it felt good. He gently squeezed her fingers and gave her courage to share.

When she told about Larry's mother she heard murmurs and some anger. Almost every one attending said they were on her side – she should ignore the woman. Except Robert. He whispered to her.

"This might me your mission from God. At least your assignment."

Melanie left the group shaken. She was there alone

tonight. No Candy, no Noelle, no Natalie. On her own. Not even Vivian the ultimate Candy Cane mother.

Robert steered her out of the room firmly holding his hand on her elbow. She was grateful for that. He led her to his car, opened the passenger door and guided her in.

So many mixed emotions. *Is this okay? Is he okay? Am I doing the right thing?*

She felt like she had no control, but in some way it felt good to not have to decide.

Robert pulled over after leaving the parking lot. It was a patch of grass, but it worked as a respite. "Sorry, Mel, but I am really worried about you. Can I, may I, help? I just want to be a friend."

Her first rational thought was, *I am in his car. Where is mine? And, he called me Mel, not Melanie.*

She tried to control her shaking, but this whole scenario was weird. She had allowed a man she hardly knew to guide her into his car and drive away with her. A man who called her by her nickname without asking. What had she been thinking?

"Mel? You're shaking." His eyes found her face and his hand tipped her chin up. "I am so sorry. Didn't mean to scare you, only help."

She nodded but knew her face was moist. Darn those tears! She must learn to control them. "I . . . it's okay. Thanks for your help. Can you drive me back to my car now?"

She started to jump quickly out of his, but he rushed to open her car door for her, since in her nervousness she had forgotten to lock it. When she turned to thank him, he shoved a business card in her hand. "Please, Mel, keep this. Please. Call me anytime day or night when you just want to talk. No obligation, just friendship. Honest." She nodded. Why did the card have a faint antiseptic smell? Maybe he had just gotten them printed. She shoved it in her purse.

Nat was waiting for her with Lola nestled between her legs on the sofa when she got home. The dog jumped up wiggling and whining and licking Mel's ankles. So much love, so much comfort. She grabbed her straggly furry friend in her arms, plopped next to Nat on the ancient sofa and hugged and cuddled. What could be better and more honest and pure than the love of a dog. She missed Larry so much. Why did he do what he did? Why did he keep his illegal dealings secret from her? It hurt so much that he hadn't trusted her, especially after he had accepted Christ and been baptized. Their wedding had been so beautiful, their love had been special. She started to turn the blue ring on her finger. It wasn't there. Gone. No longer hers.

Natalie leaned over and hugged her encircling Mel's arms that were holding Lola. "You can't go back, Mel. You mustn't go there. For the good memories, yes. But, for the painful ones, no."

BONNIE ENGSTROM

Chapter Twelve
Robert to the rescue

It was the last day of school before Spring break. Melanie had overslept and was rushing to her car parked in the apartment lot. She had been too tired and drained last night to bother with the underground garage and the habitually slow elevator. She and Nat had talked for a long time, Nat assuring her it was probably okay that Robert befriended her.

"He's probably one of those super caring, sensitive men. After all, it sounds like he probably went through hell on earth with his dying wife. He's probably just being kind." Suddenly, she burst out laughing. "I probably said probably way too much," she giggled. Mel laughed, and the two spent the next ten minutes verbally cross-examining Robert, among spurts of giggles.

Melanie couldn't resist. "You're *probably* right, Nat. He really is *probably* being kind."

That set them off again. Finally realizing the time, and since they both had to appear at work the next morning, Nat left with Lola whining at her feet. "All I have to do is pick up my keys and she whines. Am I that special to her?"

~

Late! Mel checked her face and hair in the entry mirror, grabbed a cardigan from the hall tree and rushed through the door colliding head on with Larry's mother.

"What are you doing here?"

"Came to bond with my daughter-in-law." But the smirk on her face said something else. She dropped the gray satchel at her feet and opened her arms wide. To hug?

"No way!" Mel tried to smirk back, but she had never been good at making faces – the reason she never garnered a spot in the variety show in high school when she tried so hard to be funny.

"Why are you sneering at me?" the older woman cocked her head, maybe to get a better look at Mel's features. "You have blue eyes," she said. "Larry always liked little white girls with blue eyes. Like the ocean he said."

Melanie turned to lock the front door, then remembered the hidden key in the porch light. Should she take it, too? She didn't want this obnoxious woman finding it and entering her home.

"Better take the other key so's I can't get in." The woman pointed a knarled finger with a dirty nail toward the porch light and laughed. "You should've parked in the underground garage, m'lady." She cocked her head again and squinted. "You really are a lady, ain't you? My Larry liked the finer things."

Melanie's first thought was how would the woman know what Larry liked since she left him when he was barely a toddler? She realized this was not the time to dwell on questions. She had to get out of there and go to work. Maybe a confidential chat with Ms. Dana would help, even one with Nora her co-teacher now that they were friends again. Then she remembered the card from Robert tucked in the pocket of her purse. Could he, would he, help? Fingering the raised numbers of his phone, she called as she was backing out of her space.

"The first thing you should do, Mel, is call the police and ask to have your home under surveillance. At least if this woman does try to enter, they will know your concerns before it happens. Do it right now and call me back."

He sounded so sure, so firm. She made the call. The Newport Beach Police were kind and understanding. All she had to tell them was a woman she didn't know camped on her apartment doorstep two days ago and appeared at her door again this morning. When she called him back the second thing Robert suggested was to call the apartment managing company. At a traffic signal she had time to scroll through her phone until she found it and reached a woman named Hanna.

"So glad you called and alerted us. We've had several complaints about attempted break-ins this past week. Also, a few residents who saw a homeless woman on the steps next to the street. Do you have any information, do you know who she is?"

Time to fib. Not really, because other than her insisting she is Larry's mother, I do not know who she is. She never gave me her name, so I'm telling the truth. "No, I don't know her name. Sorry."

~

The children were adorable today. Nora was a good

sport when Jackson blew his apple juice across the table. The other kids laughed. So, it was okay. It was the drive home that scared her, especially entering her apartment. But, she discovered, she wouldn't be alone.

"Surprise!" Robert stood on her doorstep and sported a Cheshire grin above his neat beard. His hands fiddled in his pockets, and his amber brown eyes had warm crinkles around them. "I hope it's okay I'm here. So glad you called me. I've been worried."

Melanie felt his warmth, couldn't deny it. It was wonderful to have a hero. Was he that? He reached his hands to hers, and she took them. Still warm, still dry and not sweaty. Still smelled of antiseptic. She chuckled to herself. Is this a way to determine if a man is honest and real? Right now she was grateful for his support. He smiled that warm smile she remembered from him sitting beside her at the grief group. She sent up a silent prayer. It was going to be all right.

"Let's check the front door first. Then the windows. Okay?"

She nodded and followed.

At the front door they found a note. "I will be back. You are mine now, and I am yours."

Melanie crumbled into Robert's arms. "What does this woman want? Her son, my husband, is dead. Doesn't she understand dead?"

"She's desperate, Mel. No, I don't think she wants to understand, just has her own agenda."

The windows were intact as well as the door to the parking garage. No one had entered her home, so she believed. Until . . . she went into the kitchen.

"How did she get in?" Melanie and Robert gazed dumfounded at all the food on the counter, and on the floor. Squashed tomatoes, half broken carrots, piles of cheese, mounds of mashed avocado, heaps of raw hamburger. Whole onions, red and white, nestled among the piles and mounds. They looked like big orbs, like a wide-eyed child asking for answers. Lola was hiding and whimpering in the laundry room. Poor baby.

"Lola," Mel whispered and picked her up. "You aren't a very good guard dog, are you?" She ruffled the mohawk tuft of white fur between the dog's ears. "Are you okay?"

This time Melanie would control her tears. She set Lola down and grabbed Robert's blue shirt sleeves and clung to them, almost shaking him out of them. She was so angry she couldn't think straight until Robert loosened himself from her grip and pulled his cellphone out of a back pocket.

"What are you doing?" she screamed. "No, no. Do not give her the satisfaction. No!"

"Too late. I already dialed 911."

Melanie slumped in a wooden kitchen chair. Finally the sobs came. She heard Robert in the laundry room talking quietly. He returned and put a warm hand on her shoulder, shook his head and pulled out another chair across the island to face her. "So sorry, Mel. So sorry you are going through this." She noticed his eyes glistened as he drew a tissue from the ever present box on the counter and dabbed at her cheeks. What did it matter anymore? That woman had won. She had invaded her home, made her point, violated Melanie. And frightened her dog.

The police sergeant, the one with the glimmering badge who handed her a business card she was too distraught to read, lifted up a camera. Just as he was about to take a photo, he stooped down.

"Did you see this?" He held up a napkin with printing on it. "No, don't touch. Unlikely to get prints, but we will try." He held the corner of the napkin with a plastic sandwich bag, even though he was wearing gloves. He practically waved it in front of her face. Melanie blinked.

The words were obviously scribbled with the gel pen she kept to make her grocery lists. The one in the little magnetic container on the side of the fridge. She heard Robert gasp.

"Oh, my gosh!"

"What? Hold it closer, please, officer." He did. She read. She ran to the bathroom to be sick.

What did that woman want from her? The words on the napkin almost haunted her.

Hungry. Will be back. Daughter-in-law.

Chapter Thirteen
Francine

Francine plopped her gray bag on the cement in front of the apartment complex. She loved that no one, not even Melanie, knew her name. Not her real name. Not even the people she had shared digs with under the bridge. Even if Larry was alive, he wouldn't know her name. She had been careful about that. So glad Larry's dad is dead. Poor man. A good guy, actually. Once. Until he threw her out.

Francine shuffled her body clad with bulk on the cement and dug through her bag finally coming up with a take-out salad in a plastic container from Melanie's fridge. Maybe a bit old, but it would do. She poured the little vessel of dressing on it, picked up the black plastic fork and speared a lettuce leaf. Not bad at all. She'd always loved Caesar salad. The croutons were soggy. That was okay. Still chewy.

Tossing the empty plastic container aside, she rubbed her stomach and burped. If only there had been chicken in the salad, it would have been perfect. Next step, get that Melanie girl to fess up. Surely, her honest son would have told her about his illegal activities. Ain't that what people in love did? She must have known.

Her finger hovered over Melanie's cell number. Just as she was about to press the green button, a police car drove up.

~

"You caught her?"

"Yes, Ma'am. She was squatting on the steps to your apartment complex. We took her in for booking."

"Oh." Melanie couldn't believe her next question to the police officer. "Is she all right?

"I mean is she safe?"

The youthful officer looked at her askew. "Do you care about this woman?"

"Yes, well, sort of." Melanie pulled a tissue from her purse and pressed it to her face. "She . . . she," she stumbled on the words. The officer tipped his head. To encourage her?

Finally, Melanie got her breath. Her gasp seemed to startle the officer. So young she thought. Probably never been through trauma and drama like this. Composing herself with effort only God could give, she explained.

"This woman, whose name I do not know, is the mother of my recently deceased husband."

Office Penney nodded. Did he really understand? Could anyone?

Chapter Fourteen
Friends

"I don't know what to do." Melanie wrung her hands like she'd seen old women do. Natalie raised her brows in question. "Should I go to her? I mean technically she is my kin, sort of. By marriage."

Nat finally spoke. Her voice was dry and raspy. She cleared her throat. Choking back tears? "Here is what I suggest. But, the call is yours, either to make or not."

"Aw, I get it. Call the others," she hesitated. "For advice and prayer." She shook her head tossing her brown curls, then shoved them back off her face with her fingers. "So embarrassing, but so needed." She dialed the first number, then the code for the others – Cindy in Costa Rica and Connie in Arizona. Finally, they were all on. A minute of confusion ensued. Nat grabbed the phone and calmed all the other Candy Canes down. Nat explained, Melanie chimed in. After almost an hour there was a lot of crying and prayer.

Candy finally spoke. "I was there when this woman tried to confront Mel in Starbucks. I didn't trust her then, and I don't trust her now."

Candy's mom Vivian must have grabbed the phone. When she spoke all the girls quieted.

"Thank you, ladies, for letting me interfere and put my old two cents in," she chuckled. Nat who knew her so well could almost see Candy elbowing her mom. She giggled, and many of the other women did, too.

"I have been praying for you, Mel, for guidance," the older woman said. "I asked the Holy Spirit for direction. I've been led to the Scripture in Psalm 85:13 *Righteousness goes before him and prepares the way for his steps.* The message I got is that this woman is your mission. God led her to you for a very specific reason. Your steps will prepare the way for her healing and her salvation. Sorry, but I feel strongly about this."

Melanie gasped. "That's exactly what Robert said, that this woman might be my mission. How could that be?"

That set off a cacophony of voices. "Who is Robert? Explain."

Mel passed the phone to Natalie and collapsed on the old sofa. How could she explain? How could they possibly understand?

Nat took over, explained the grief group situation hoping everyone would understand. A collective sigh from five other women. "Oh, got it." "Poor Mel." Finally, "We are here for you, girl."

Mel ran to the bathroom and splashed cold water on her face. Makeup ruined, but so what? When she came back she took the phone from Natalie. All she could say was, "Thanks."

Chapter Fifteen
Melanie

Robert was standing outside the room. He reached for her hands. She shook her head keeping her hands at her side. She wanted his touch but was afraid it would be a commitment. "Thanks, I am okay." That was the best she could do. She had driven here alone without support of friends. Maybe again she could do this on her own. But, Robert was her friend, wasn't he?

Pulling a hand from his pocket he touched her elbow and led her in to the room, the room where she would have to share more grief, the room where she must go beyond herself.

BONNIE ENGSTROM

Chapter Sixteen
Who, what?

It was one of those rare balmy days in Southern California. Francine lifted her face to the wind and sucked in the cool breeze. If she had stayed in Arizona it would have been dry and drier. Almost summer with overwhelming heat, no relief. Unless one had a car with AC, or better yet a house. Ha! Fat chance for that unless that selfish girl who married her Larry gave up and helped her.

Somebody had bailed her out. She really didn't care who, just that it happened. Still, she wondered. Was it 'that' girl? The one who her son married? Naw, that girl hated her, and for good reason. Who was it? Why?

~

Melanie checked her online bank account. It went through. Still, she wondered why she had done this for a woman who was so confrontational, a woman who had abandoned her child at a young age. A woman who must hate her, and yet who felt entitled.

Both Candy's husband Will and Connie's husband,

Jaeda, had suggested she should consult a lawyer. It was frightening that Larry's mother was focusing on her. Didn't the woman understand Melanie had nothing? No death benefits. No inheritance? Nothing she'd had before she married Larry, except the blue diamond ring. Now, she no longer had that.

She called Randi, but Randi explained she only took family law cases. Wasn't this family law? After all, the woman was basically her mother-in-law, or was until Larry died. Why, why had that new strain of influenza spread through the prison? Larry had had his flu shot, Melanie made sure. But, as Randi reminded her, it hadn't covered everything, and medical care in prison was much less than desired. So . . . Larry died.

He had been a big strong man, a man who exercised and took care of this health. Just not enough.

Melanie wanted to get back to normal. But, first she needed legal protection from that woman. It would never be normal when the hostile woman was camping on the stoop imposing on her privacy. Tonight was the grief group. Maybe she could share there, if she was brave enough.

She walked in alone. This time Robert spotted her and stood up. He set down his cup of coffee and spread out his arms. She welcomed his friendship and hoped it was just that. Connie's husband Jaeda, the online computer guru, had looked him up for her, said he was bona fide, one hundred percent honest. She had sensed that, as had Candy, but she wanted to be sure since Robert was becoming a support system and a friend. He led her to a seat next to him and squeezed her hand lightly. Then, she spoke and her world collapsed.

Chapter Seventeen
Support

Melanie swooned in Natalie's and Candy's arms. Vivian was there, too. Robert was holding her hand still. They had all gathered in Mel's apartment, but she wasn't sure why the other Candy Canes were there.

"I called them, Mel. Got their numbers from your cellphone when you were speaking, before you passed out. Sorry. It was an invasion of privacy." He bowed his head and let go of Mel's hands to shove his fiddling into the pockets of his khakis. "I thought you needed support from your friends. Candy Canes was a group name on your caller list."

Should she hug him or smack him? She wasn't sure how to react to his confession. Still, she had her Candy Cane sisters here to support her and listen to her woes, and most importantly, pray.

~

Robert closed the door behind him after giving Melanie a hug. Would she hear a huge sigh of relief? He thought she might since he was relieved to be out of there. He wasn't sure why he had befriended Melanie so much. She had seemed so fragile, so lost. Yet, he envied her support system, all those girls, all that friendship, even a mom figure.

When Dartha died he'd only had his brother. Not a believer. Yet, Ron had been by his side. Not during the dying process, but after at the funeral and the burial. Ron had actually flung his arm around Robert's shoulders and whispered, "So sorry," in his ears. That had been more than expected, and very welcomed. It helped.

Robert couldn't imagine having a support system like Melanie had, like the Candy Canes. He wished he could join the group. But, it was exclusive to women. Newport Beach swim women. Then he remembered hearing about a man named Jaeda who was married to one of the women. Was there a way to be part of it? Who was this man? Was there a way he could contact him?

~

Melanie wasn't sure when she got the text from Robert asking to be connected to the other Candy Cane men who were married to the special group of girls? It was a bizarre request. Before she honored it she needed to ask the girls and Jaeda and Rob and Braydon and Bill and Will. Such a heavy request. Should she? Was it up to her, her responsibility?

She contacted the women first for their opinions. They of course asked their husbands. Rob and Will weren't so sure, but good old Jaeda and Braydon and Bill, Senior seemed okay with it. She was a little disturbed about Will since Candy had been so supportive of her by coming to the Starbucks and the grief group. Still, it was his choice, and she knew Candy would pray about it. Rob was so out of the loop living in Costa Rica struggling with Cindy to start a church and raising an infant son, as well as conducting AA meetings and MS support groups. She wasn't surprised he'd said, "Not now. Sorry." She knew he and Cindy were overwhelmed with the responsibilities of their life. Finally, she decided to connect Robert with Braydon first. "If you are still willing," she texted.

"I am," he responded. "But, I think you should hook him up with Bill. He is the senior member of the men in this group, the wisest."

After confirming with Bill that he was still open to communication with Robert, she sent Robert his email. What she hadn't expected was Robert's anxiousness. The next day Vivian asked Melanie, "Aren't grief groups supposed to be confidential?" That's when Melanie knew, when she started to worry about her so-called friendship with Robert. From now on she would be careful of every word she spoke in grief group. At least she planned to be.

Chapter Eighteen
Decisions

What was Robert up to? He had suddenly become part of her life, and she wasn't sure she was ready for that, nor wanted it. Nice guy, kind, considerate and caring. But what were his reasons? Did he have a motive? He had consistently held her hand before she spoke at the grief meetings, walked her to her car, seemed to care. Too much? Could she trust that?

She finally had the courage to confront him after this meeting. She told him how much she appreciated his support, "But, Robert, I'm not ready for a relationship." He nodded, squeezed her elbow and walked away. She stood there alone.

~

First, she called Bill, Senior, the patriarch of the Candy Canes. Because she could never resist being left out, Vivian got on an extension phone. It was gratifying to know they both cared, but she had wanted to talk with Bill alone.

"It's okay, Mel. Vivian and I have no secrets, and" he said, "we will both be confidential. Share away."

Melanie did. She wasn't sure why her heart sored, but Bill's and Vivian's words took root and gave her reason to be consoled. She, they said, must never feel guilty about Larry's deception or death. She'd had no control over that. Only God did. Still, there was the situation with his homeless mother.

"Mel, dear, have you tried to forgive her?" Vivian asked.

"Not sure it's my place to forgive."

"It doesn't matter, Mel. It's always our place to forgive, even," she added, "if the sin wasn't against us. God honors our faithfulness."

Mel nodded, then realized neither Bill nor Vivian could see her. Could they hear the rattling in her head? Finally, she spoke. "Thank you for your wisdom. I know you are right. It's very difficult."

"I know, dear. I will be praying for you – hard and long. Remember the passage in Psalms." Vivian was such an encourager. The quasi mom for all the girls. She hung up and dialed her own mom's number.

~

"Honey, what's wrong. I can tell by your voice," Susan said. "I know that tone."

"I love you, Mom, and I need to share. Need advice."

Melanie and Susan had endured so much from Bruce, her step father and Susan's now ex-husband. It had finally ended when he was arrested for incidents they didn't want to know about when he was the principal at Vista del Mar High School. He had accosted Noelle in the parking lot and she was able to get away from him, and in her fear she almost ran him over. Then the front office receptionist had reported him when she found incriminating slips of paper in his waste basket, enough to send him to jail. Both were finally free of him. Now, Melanie was dealing with another agonizing situation. At least Bruce had been alive and in front of her. Larry was dead. And, his mother wouldn't let her forget it.

Maybe she did need Robert's support.

~

Susan punched the button on her cell phone. She was tempted to fling it across the room. Unfortunately, that wouldn't erase the conversation or help her daughter make a decision. She hoped she had given her good advice, and especially emotional support. The Robert man sounded sincere and caring. But she and Melanie had been fooled before, especially by Bruce.

She called Mel back. "Idea! How about inviting him to dinner at my house?" The silence on the other end was almost devastating. Long, too long.

~

"Your mother wants to meet me?"

Melanie released her hand from his as they were leaving the grief group and walking to their cars. She nodded. Slightly.

"Why?"

"Because that's what moms do, Robert."

"Oh. She cares." His voice dropped. "Never had one who cared that much."

"You must have had some love since your brother came to your wife's funeral." It was more a question than a statement, but Mel hoped it would do. And make sense to him.

"Yeh. But the caring was as siblings, not learned from parents."

Melanie's heart almost broke from that, but she pressed on. "Did you ever contact Bill?"

His eyes brightened, and he actually grinned. "Great guy! Said to come over any time to chat with him. Maybe I'll do that soon."

"Why not tonight? You can ask him about doing dinner at my mom's. What he thinks about it." She scurried to her car without waiting for an answer. As she turned the key in the ignition she saw Robert out of the corner of her eye . . . still standing. Decisions must be difficult for him. But, she knew Bill and how he would mentor, how he would instill confidence, and faith. She hoped Robert would call Bill and receive that gift.

Chapter Nineteen
Questions

Vivian spread her arms and embraced Robert. He took a step back and managed to grin.

"So glad you came, Robert," Bill said. His smile was genuine and the slap on the shoulder comforting in a manly manner. "Sorry Viv is so demonstrative. She loves company."

Robert noticed the funny expression on his hostess's face. She didn't seem angry, more teasing. He laughed. "I was taken back a bit, just didn't expect such a warm welcome." He offered his jacket to Vivian to hang up and settled in the chair Bill indicated. "But, I loved it.

"I want to get to know you both, to know Melanie's friends." He picked at a piece of lint or something on his knee. "Losing Larry and how he deceived her has been a huge struggle for her. Even with her faith," he added.

"Yes, we know," Bill said. "But we can't change what happened." He looked Robert in the face. "We were there, at the wedding. Did you know that?"

Robert shook his head. "No idea. So, you knew it was a sudden marriage? That they barely knew each other before the wedding?" He fumbled with the lint on his knee. Looking up at Bill he asked the dreaded question about the woman he was falling in love with. "Was she so desperate . . . for marriage and for love?"

Chapter Twenty
Anger

Melanie slammed the door and threw her work tennies against the hall mirror. "Shatter! Shatter! Please." When it didn't she banged her fists on the glaring glass. "What was wrong with me? Why didn't I use my brain instead of my heart? Why was I so foolish, so desperate for love?" Sobbing into her cupped hands she dropped on the sofa, cradled Lola in her arms and called Natalie.

"I was stupid, wasn't I?" she begged. "I let my heart and my need overcome good sense." She shook her head even though Nat couldn't see it. "I was truly stupid, and desperate to fall in love with Larry. Larry the liar.

"And now I have Larry the liar's lying mother to deal with. Why, Nat, why?"

~

Nat held Melanie sobbing and shaking in her arms. She had closed up the gym in record time and rushed to her friend. She was worried. Worried about Melanie's health, mostly mental. The girl had gone through so much in so little time. Was this a breaking point?

57

Natalie had declared psychology as her minor in college, but that didn't count, not really. She had skimmed through the classes and the tests, barely making a C minus. No, she needed more expert advice to help Mel.

~

Robert? No way. Nat couldn't believe it. She was back home and checked again on the Google site. Melanie's Robert? The one who supported her during the grief groups? So, he was a counselor, a therapist with accolades, even many positive Yelp reviews. How could that be? Did Melanie know? She needed to. Or, maybe not.

Natalie called Bill and Vivian for advice. Because they were her elders? Or, because they were substitute parents. Either way she trusted their wisdom.

"No way should she know," Bill said adamantly. "At least not yet. It would intimidate her. She might think he was always analyzing her, like she was a patient, and he was trying to save her."

"I disagree," Vivian grabbed the phone. It seemed to be her modus operandi. Nat laughed to herself. That Vivian! The older woman talked on. "She needs to know. Right now she is ignorant, out of the loop. What if she finds out later and believes he hasn't told her for the wrong reason? Then she will mistrust him." She took a breath. Nat heard the sigh. Vivian went on. "Besides, there is the mother-in-law issue. She needs help to deal with that strange woman." She took another deep breath. "I don't want to call her evil, but I'm coming close."

Nat nodded her head that they couldn't see, thanked them and hung up the phone.

In the end it didn't matter. Robert made the decision for them during dinner at Susan's.

BONNIE ENGSTROM

Chapter Twenty-one
Dinner

Susan Carson hummed to her favorite praise song as she set the table. It will be fun to meet Melanie's new friend. Poor girl was so deceived by that Larry. She stopped clutching a napkin to her breast and remembered the love she saw in Larry and Mel's eyes during their wedding vows. She had been privileged to be her daughter's matron of honor and hold the exquisite blue diamond ring tucked in her bouquet. No, that was Natalie as maid of honor. She had wanted to, but Mel chose Nat. Oh, well – didn't matter now. Ring was gone. Forever.

She folded the napkin in a triangle shape and placed it next to the last plate. Once again she wished she had watched the video about how to fold napkins in special shapes. Not that she entertained much anymore. That was the one, the only thing, she missed about marriage to her ex-husband Bruce. He did love to entertain. Mostly for his gain. She remembered the senator, the city manager, the school superintendent. She doubted if any of them remembered Bruce, and certainly not her. Certainly not her gourmet dinners.

The doorbell chimed while she was checking the oven. Thank goodness for oven mitts or she would have burned her fingers when the bell startled her. She set the casserole on top of the stove and raced to the door. Why on earth was Melanie ringing the bell instead of using her key?

She swung the door open and gasped. A bedraggled, disheveled woman layered in dirty clothes stared back at her. What smelled she wondered, the clothes or the woman?

"Hi, sweetie. Am I late? I heard you are having a party, and I'm starved."

Susan tried to slam the door, but a booted foot prevented it. The woman shoved her way in, pushed past Susan almost knocking her over and deposited her strangely clad body on the sofa. Susan knew instantly who she was but asked the rhetorical question anyway. "Who are you?"

The woman clasped her belly and let out a stream of laughter. Finally, wiping her nose on her hand and then the hand on her tattered skirt, she spoke. "Name's Francine. But you probably knew that already. I, sweetie, am the other mother." She squinted at Susan and laughed again. "The one whose son paid for the ring that belongs now to me."

Would this woman never stop laughing? Susan was sure she was inebriated or on drugs or something. She decided to be firm. "Get out of here. You are not invited. Get out," she screamed, "or I am calling the police."

Raucous laughter echoed the room. The woman didn't budge. Susan picked up her cellphone to dial

911.

"No! Stop! No police. Just give me some food. I will leave and not disturb your fancy dinner."

Susan filled a Tupperware container with lots of the casserole, poured ice tea into a disposable cup, put all in a two-handled Trader Joe's paper bag with plastic utensils and napkins. Would this woman even use them or just shovel the food into her mouth with her scrawny hands? She thrust the whole business into the brown hands just before Melanie and her friend Robert walked in.

~

"I can't believe she did that, Mom. And, that you gave her food. You really should have called the police. You know she's already been arrested."

"I know. I had my fingers on the buttons when she begged me to stop. I know Jesus said the poor will always be with us. I decided to give her food so maybe she would go away."

"She won't Mrs. Carson, now that you've accepted her." Robert spoke up. "Sorry I didn't introduce myself before. No chance." He laughed, pulled his hand out of his pocket and reached for Susan's hand.

"My fault, Robert. So glad you could come. I'm anxious to get to know you, my Melanie's new friend." Robert nodded, but it was a strange nod.

~

"The casserole was delicious, the salad crisp and the desert divine."

"Gosh, Robert, you sound like an advertisement." Melanie wiped the last remnant of the dinner off her mouth and placed her napkin on the table. "I will help Mom clean up. You go into the den and vegge out.

Coffee coming soon."

Melanie noticed Robert clasping his hands together, wringing them. Hard? Strange, because he was usually so relaxed around her. She set the tray of coffee and Costco Macaroons down on the coffee table in front of him. "They are just tidbits. No need to take any if you don't want," she said. He nodded, but his eyes looked misty. Strange. He was always so strong when he supported her during and after the grief meetings. Was he having second thoughts about their friendship? She sensed he was about to reveal something.

Chapter Twenty-two
Revelation

"You didn't know?"

Susan held Melanie's hand. Robert had left and they had turned off the Netflix episode of Call the Midwife. Such a wonderful drama, but so intense. Especially now.

"Nope. Never thought to ask. I figured he was a business type guy, maybe in real estate. Never occurred to me he was a shrink. He gave me his card, but I never looked closely at it."

"Well, Mel, his profession could either be a blessing or a curse. What do you think? I choose blessing." She had answered her own question but was waiting for Melanie to answer it.

"I was shocked, but when I thought it through it made sense. He had a special way of relating to me." Mel squeezed Susan's hand tighter. "I don't know, Mom. What I do know is I like him. A lot. And he seems to genuinely care for me." She looked into Susan's eyes, the wise eyes of her mother. "I . . . I think I care for him, too. Too soon, huh?"

~

Melanie struggled out of her bed sheets and stumbled to the floor. Who was banging on her door at five a.m.? She almost ignored it hoping it was a mistake or a bad dream. But, the tall man in the blue uniform confirmed it wasn't. He had Larry's mother in the grip of his arm. She was slumped over, eyes almost closed, the hand on her free arm clutching the dirty gray satchel by her side.

Officer Watkins produced a card that Mel took with a shaky hand. "Do you know this person?" he asked. "She says she is a relative. Found her camped again on the sidewalk. Gave your name and apartment number." His words all seemed to jumble together. Melanie shook her head. She was only half awake, if that. What was the despicable woman doing here . . . again.

"No, officer, she is not a relative."

"Melanie, it's me. Francine. Larry's mother." Then, "Please, please."

"So, you do know her?" Watkins said.

"Not really. I only know 'of' her. She has been stalking me."

"If that's so, you should make a report and get a protection agreement, you know, a restraining order."

"Good advice, officer. Maybe I will. Thanks." Melanie closed the door and ran to the bathroom gagging. Why was Larry's mother harassing her? She had nothing to give her. The ring was gone. He had no insurance, only a dented car that the police had towed away and a cheap apartment. Nothing.

~

Melanie stood in line. How could there be a line to

file for a restraining order? She looked at the people behind her and in front of her, almost all women except for one elderly man. Poor soul. Was he a victim of elder abuse? She would never know, but she prayed for him. She noticed almost all the women either wore long sleeves, or those who didn't had bruises on their arms, even bruises over tattoos. One had a purple ring of yellow around her eye. She was clutching a small child by the hand. Another child nearly pulled his mother's tee shirt off he grasped it so tightly. Melanie almost stepped out of line, then changed her mind. There were many reasons she realized for filing a protection agreement. Not all were because of physical abuse. Stalking and harassing surely counted, too. Finally, it was her turn. The woman behind the desk asked her for the name of the person she was filing against. All she knew was Francine. Had she kept her married name? If so it was the same as Larry's. Why hadn't the nice officer given her more direction? Maybe because he isn't a lawyer? Apparently, she could explain and just give a description. So, that's what she did. She prayed it would work.

~

Natalie hugged her, then got right up in her face. "You need a lawyer."

"For what? I haven't done anything wrong."

"For guidance and protection." She paused and wiped her hands on her gym pants. "I know they aren't cheap, but really Mel, you need legal advice. Call Randi. Please."

So, she did.

~

Randi nodded. Approval? "Glad I had a spare half

hour. Sit down. We can make this quick."

Randi would go to the hearing with Mel to affirm the need for a protection agreement. "Least I can do. You need representation."

She also agreed Melanie had done the right thing. This Francine woman was a menace. Maybe even a threat. But, why did Melanie feel sorry for her?

Chapter Twenty-three
Protection

It was a done deal. Melanie wondered how tired the judges must get hearing all these reasons for restraining orders. Fortunately, not her problem, their job. Still, it was weird going before a judge and explaining why she needed protection from an old lady. An old lady who was now legally prevented from coming within a hundred feet of her. How she wondered would that prevent Francine from camping on the curb outside the apartment complex? Still, it was something, and the woman couldn't come to her door anymore. Then she wondered, how would Francine even know about the restraining order? Unless she again camped on the curb and the police were called. Hopefully, another resident would do that. It was too much to take in. She needed to share this with Robert. Surely, he would understand.

~

"I don't understand. Why did you do this? That poor woman must be desperate, and homeless. Maybe you are her only salvation."

Melanie would have slapped him if she could over the phone line. Didn't he understand she was afraid of the woman? Didn't he remember how she had broken into her home and threw food all over the kitchen?

"I don't understand, Robert," she said through gritted teeth. "I got the impression you cared about me . . . as a friend," she added in a whisper. "Yes, I feel sorry for her, but she has disrupted my life, even threatened me."

Silence.

"Well?" She wasn't sure why she hadn't hung up. This man was unfeeling, not the man she thought he was. Her finger was on the red button when he spoke.

"I . . . I don't know either. Sorry."

She hung up.

Melanie was angry, but not sure who with. Obviously Robert, the turncoat, but a little with herself, too. Natalie always had wisdom to share. Maybe she should call her.

~

Natalie wasn't sure how to respond. She knew the woman had invaded Mel's home and even threatened her. Now, she was conflicted. She, too, like Robert had a soft spot for the homeless, even kept a few five dollar bills in her car console to hand out the passenger window. Especially to the ones who had dog companions. She had even bought a bag of kibbles for one young man who accepted it gratefully. His dog, Cassius, he told her its name was after the famous fighter, leaped toward the bag and pawed it. They both laughed when she said, "He knows something is in there for him."

"Everything is for him," the good-looking man said. She thought about him often. He was movie star handsome, young. Not like so many of the grizzled, bearded old guys who anchored the street corners. If she had met him in any other circumstance she would have been tempted to date him. He was courteous and engaging, and way too young and clean cut to be homeless standing on the corner next to her supermarket. She thought of him often. Maybe he had been dropped off as a pawn on one of the buses that drove homeless people around to places where they could get the most donations. She had to let his handsome face go. No good would come of thinking of him. Oh, desperate for love . . . again?

"I think you did the right thing, Mel. You needed closure. You need to get this woman out of your life."

"You think so? Robert doesn't. He thinks I'm an uncaring, self-centered person."

"Mel, I know you. I know you aren't that way at all. Remember, Robert doesn't know you. He doesn't know your history, all you've gone through. He probably doesn't have a grasp on your faith, either." Nat stopped talking and thought. Was she telling Melanie the right thing? She wanted Mel protected from a crazy woman. But, was the woman really crazy, or just desperate? She left a small child when he was only a toddler with a husband who was also mostly absent. What effect had that had on Larry? Surely, that must have had something to do with Larry being deceptive. She didn't want Mel caught up in more deception. From her own experience with Bryce who had left her injured on the ground after an aborted sky dive, deception fostered more deception. No, she would support Mel in trying to keep that weird and intrusive woman away from her. But, if Larry had lived, the woman would be her mother-in-law.

BONNIE ENGSTROM

Chapter Twenty-four
Sharing

It was such a beautiful night he almost didn't want to go. Robert had been to so many grief groups over too many years as both a grieving husband and a counselor still wanting to learn. He didn't often check the night sky, but tonight was exceptional. There was a full moon glowing and stars sparkling. Unique in usually cloudy southern California. His father had been an amateur astronomer and taught him as a young boy how to look for the Big Dipper and a few constellations. He had never pursued it but was still in awe of God's heavens. The firmament was a dark almost cerulean and for once unencumbered by haze or ocean fog. The stars glittered in the unusually clear coastal sky. He found the Big Dipper, and that satisfied him. He wiped off his hand, opened his car door and started the engine.

How would she be tonight, if she came? Would she be at least cordial? He knew he had blown it during their brief phone conversation. He hadn't known how to explain to her why he felt so strongly about the desperate woman who had come into her life.

~

Melanie entered the circle hesitantly. She saw only one empty chair. Next to Robert. She had hoped not to sit next to him tonight. She had even prayed about it briefly, but she guessed God had other plans. She walked slowly to the empty chair and sat. Robert shifted a bit toward her. She wondered what God was thinking.

Robert smiled and reached for her hand, but she kept both of hers buried in the folds of her skirt, the blue one, the one she called God-colored. He shook his head slightly and barely whispered, "Sorry." She shrugged. His heart sank. Wasn't she going to acknowledge him at all? He folded his own hands and hooked one over a crossed knee. Two could play this game. His foot, the one attached to the hand-hooked knee, decided to jiggle. Then it beat a cadence in the air. Ugh. Wasn't supposed to do that, except when nervous.

"Guess what, Bobby?" He could hear his mother's saccharine voice in his head. He was nine years old. She was chastising him, sort of, and trying to help him, but it hadn't worked. Backfired instead. "Nervous tic is what you have." He had shaken his head. Denial was easy at nine. "Yes, son, you do. You need to learn how to control it. Very distracting." She had placed a hand on the bouncing leg and squeezed. But, the bouncing didn't stop, only escalated. The warmth of her hand didn't help, especially not the squeeze. "What," she said, "if you are in a very important situation? Like getting an award, or sitting in the principal's office to defend yourself for a wrong doing?" She had grabbed his shoulders firmly and turned him to face her, to look him in the eyes. "This nervous tic, this bouncing leg thing, will make you look terrified. Gotta stop it, Bobby. Now."

He had. Prayer had helped a lot. He memorized Philippians 4:13 and repeated it each time his leg quivered. *I can do all things through Christ who strengthens me.* He remembered that from Sunday school classes, the ones he'd been forced to go to, then loved under the tutelage of kind teachers. It had become his favorite verse, so he said it now in his head twenty-six years later. He could re-develop a friendship with Melanie. He could share his love for her to her. He settled in, barely hearing the other members' stories. He waited for Melanie's, again. His knee stopped jiggling.

~

She wanted to smack herself. Why was she repeating the same old story? By now everyone knew about Larry, about his deception and their flawed, flagrant marriage. Well, maybe not the new woman in the group with the dreadlocks. Maybe because she was black she would have some insight, some empathy. Melanie chastised herself. What did color have to do with it? So stupid. After sharing again, for the umpteenth time, she apologized. The woman next to her, another black one, not the new one, put her arm around Mel's shoulder and hugged. Robert just nodded and smiled.

Melanie was exhausted, drained. This session was over the top. She had shared too much, way too much, again. When she finally finished her allotted time, she was embarrassed. She felt her cheeks heat up, and she covered her eyes with damp hands. Why had she told about the homeless woman? She was not part of her grief. Not, technically.

Chapter Twenty-five
Idea

She was there again sitting on the curb in front of the large apartment complex. What was her name, the name she told Susan? Francine? Seemed like a funny made-up name to Melanie. Too fancy for a homeless woman who had abandoned her child. Not her call, God's.

Mel parked her car in the underground garage hoping to avoid the smoke from the heap of rags flicking a cigarette. She almost made it to the elevator when she felt the grip on her shoulder. "Get away from me! Go away." Melanie elbowed the woman almost knocking her over. The woman backed away cursing. That's when Melanie noticed how fragile she was. She was clothed in so many layers she looked heavy, but she wasn't. The layers hung on her, and when she turned to go, Mel could see the flimsy frame. Twig legs, body mostly bones. Clothes hanging limply. Her Larry's mother was a stick figure.

"Why do I care?" she asked Natalie during her phone call. "Am I responsible for her?"

"Not on your life, girl. But, there is a connection." She took a deep breath that Mel heard. A breath that worried her. Nat never did that unless she was going to make a big statement. "I know, and understand, why you want to cut the cord on this. Oops, bad analogy. But, have you thought about why she has been thrown into your life?" Another deep breath. "Suddenly?"

Melanie rubbed her arms. A comforting way to soothe herself. Something she had done as a little girl when her real dad had died. She needed soothing now. She knew she needed prayer. She called the other Candy Canes on the special phone line so they could all talk and pray together. Best thing she had done in a long time. She needed their support, but what would they say about her fear of the woman named Francine and . . . Robert?

~

They finally all got connected by the special phone line, even Cindy and Rob in Costa Rica. It was so good to hear their voices. Candy was driving, but fortunately had a Blue Tooth connection in her car. They could hear Connie passing the twins to Jaeda – "Your turn." Then Noel sighing. They could almost see her holding her belly filled with baby. In a few months there would be another child in the group. Doreen was closing up Winning Designs for the day, and Natalie was huddled beside Melanie in her apartment. They tried doing face time, but it got confusing and they all looked sort of weird. That set them off laughing.

"Hey, gals, Mel has some serious stuff to bring up, needs your advice and prayers," Nat said. "Calm down and listen."

The sudden silence, only breathing, scared Melanie. Could she explain? Maybe she should have written a group email. She was an expert at explaining to three-year-olds, but that was in person, even when food was being thrown across the snack table. She took a deep breath just when Candy's mother Vivian got on the line.

"Sorry, friends," Candy said somewhat contritely. "Just stopped by Mom's for something and she grabbed the phone." They all laughed and it broke the tension.

"Sorry, girls," Vivian said, but she didn't sound contrite. "I know you have something special to discuss, but I want to bring up something I've been thinking about a lot lately."

"Mom, please, not now." Candy must be wrestling the phone from Vivian. They could hear the soft scuffle and a few beeps when random buttons were accidently pressed.

"Okay. Later. Sorry." Vivian's voice disappeared.

"Sorry, too," Candy said. "You know Mom when she gets an idea in her head."

"It's okay. I for one would really like to know about her idea." Maybe listening to Vivian would delay her own appeal, one she was still reluctant to share. "Candy, bring her back," Mel requested. "Please."

"Mom, they want to hear your idea. But, please make it brief." Mel envisioned Candy leading Vivian by the elbow into the kitchen and pushing her on a counter stool. Then, they heard the exaggerated sigh. Mel, and she thought probably the other girls, had to suppress a giggle. Vivian was such a sweetheart, but she did tend to be a bit overly dramatic.

"Okay. Sorry to interrupt your discussion, but I know what it's about." Melanie could almost see Vivian's raised eyebrows and slight smile. How did she know? Maybe Susan? The two women had become friends after the horrible Bruce stalking incident.

"Here goes," Vivian said in a shaky voice. "Maybe a crazy idea. At least, think about it."

Chapter Twenty-six
Concerns

No longer called The Candy Canes? How could that be? That had been their moniker for over fifteen years. Almost everyone in Newport Beach knew them as that, recognized the name as the swim team girls in the red-striped suits who prayed. Together.

Did it sound childish as Vivian suggested? Did it sound teenagerish?

Connie said she remembered when she applied for the designer job at Nature's Designs that Doug her boss asked, "You one of 'those' girls? That crazy group?" She'd held her head high and explained the relationships. That had seemed to satisfy him when he saw her sketches.

"I . . . I'm not sure," Natalie said, although her voice wavered.

"It's not really an official title," Doreen spoke up.

"Sort of our own made-up group name," Cindy said weakly in the phone line from Costa Rica. "Actually, what Coach Beckworth called us."

"What brought this on all of a sudden, Mom?" Candy sounded annoyed, maybe angry.

Silence. Throat clearing. An abrupt booming voice. Bill?

"Guess I was out of line, girls. Presumptuous. So sorry." He cleared his throat and coughed. "Not my place. Not at all."

The girls, now women, blew a collective sigh of relief. It flew along the phone lines like a mockingbird chirping its insistent morning announcement. So, it was Bill who prompted Vivian. None of them knew why he had such power, except one, and she wasn't telling. Only she knew how he and his group of investors had saved her business. Her husband did too. But, that was their secret, and Bill's.

"We okay now?" Melanie asked.

"I hope," Doreen said.

"Me, too," Noelle echoed.

Natalie surprised them with, "I like the idea."

Candy threw in, "Another one of Mom's festering thoughts. Ugh. No way should we change our image.

"Let's get on with why Melanie called. It's important to her, and," she added quietly, "maybe to all of us."

Melanie cleared her throat but no words came out. Natalie handed her a cold bottle of water. Still nothing. Had God made her mute? She wanted advice, wanted to share, but the words wouldn't come. She elbowed Nat and gestured to the phone.

"Looks like it's up to me, girls, to tell you Mel's problem. Mostly, her indecision. Her dilemma."

Ten minutes later Nat asked, "Did I do okay?" She understood Mel was traumatized. All the other women understood, too.

"What a tough situation," Noelle said. "Not the same but reminds me of decisions I had to make when Bruce stalked me."

"We have homeless people here, too, in Costa Rica," Cindy offered. "But nothing like you have, and," she sighed, "none who invade our space."

"I want to address the Robert situation," Doreen said firmly. "I don't see the problem liking him, even trusting him. What's up with that, Mel? Come clean." Doreen was always a bit confrontational, but Natalie appreciated that side of her. After all, she was the one with the shorter leg and the limp. The one who had overcome her physical disabilities that Melanie had caused. Such a forgiving friend.

The others could hear Mel sobbing. Finally she spoke. Her voice was raspy and clogged with tears. "I feel so conflicted. Since Larry deceived me I don't know who to trust. But," she muddled, "I do feel an obligation to help his mother. Strange as she is," she added with a snuffle.

Doreen spoke again. She was the strong one, the forgiving one. "I don't see a problem helping her. Larry is dead." She probably bowed her head, but none of the others could see, except the few still on Facetime.

"But," Noelle the wary one said, "is the woman trying to scam her?"

"Probably." Nat said. "But, Mel has nothing to give her financially. She has already paid bail for her to get her out of the clinker." The all laughed at that label from their parents' era. Maybe even from their grandparents.

"Ugh, yeh, I have my car." Mel's voice trembled

again. "I don't know what to do. I want to be a good Christian and help those in need, but . . . I really don't like this woman."

Doreen's voice took over again. "Somehow, we got sidetracked. We still have not tackled the Robert situation, the one that worries me more than the homeless woman."

"You are right!" Nat's and Mel's voices chimed in unison.

"Then," Doreen said, "let's do it!"

Chapter Twenty-seven
History

Melanie was drained, exhausted. She wondered about the wisdom of calling all the girls, together. Maybe she should have called them individually or sent emails. What had she been thinking? It was time to make decisions, time to grow up. Maybe Vivian had a good idea.

Some days she felt like a teenager with friends she could laugh with and confide in. After all, she held a responsible job as a lead preschool teacher. Yes, tiny kids. But, it was important. Hadn't studies said the most important years in a child's brain development were three to six. Or, was it two to five? Either way, she held an important role in child development teaching three-year-olds.

She picked up Lola and snuggled her close. Her long tongue licked Mel's chin and her loving eyes locked with Mel's. Was that what she needed, all she needed, the love of a dog?

~

It was Thursday again. Another week had passed since the last grief session. She would love to skip tonight, but she had made a promise to herself, and to Randi. And to Natalie. Actually, she reasoned, to all the girls because they had encouraged her during the phone conversation.

Connie had said, "You are going to keep going, Mel. Please."

"You must, Mel." Candy interjected.

"You can't stop now," Cindy said. "Not until you have your feelings for the mother-in-law and Robert resolved." Cindy had a way of touching on the heart of the matter. "Don't give up now, Mel."

But, it was Doreen, the one who had forgiven the most, who clinched it. She was the one who started the prayer they all chimed in on. Melanie had to do this, if not for herself, for Doreen whose life she had altered when she had driven the red truck those years ago. She had been so graciously forgiven, maybe it was her turn now. But, how was she to forgive a woman who had abandoned her child over thirty years ago? A woman she knew nothing about, nor why she did it. A woman who by bringing that child into life gave Melanie a grasp of happiness over three decades later. She thought of Larry's portrayal of his mother that night over a glass of wine, maybe too many, but they had gotten so close, shared so much. He remembered her as gentle. She had a warm touch, and she held him close every night while tucking him into bed and kissing him on the forehead. Then, she was gone. No touches, no kisses, no lilac smell. No explanation. Only a little boy's lingering memories.

His Da had done the best he could, but he didn't have the touch of a mother. He'd visited every day when Larry was in prison for his first offense as a teenager. It was a long drive from Phoenix to Florence, but Da did it. Even paid the paltry bail that first time. After the second time he only came once a week. After the third, once a month. Then the visits stopped after the fourth time. Larry was on his own. He got a fine job, even with his teen prison record. He had been honest on his application, and he was confident and handsome. The security company hired him and gave him the role of training others, as well as choosing whom he could hire.

The tattoos she learned were mostly all from prison. She couldn't fathom that but had decided to not question or make it a big deal. He was rehabilitated, an upstanding citizen, a hard worker who had risen to a management position with a good salary and benefits. Most importantly, he was hers. He loved her and treated her with respect and dignity, and lots of kisses.

But, old habits die hard.

BONNIE ENGSTROM

Chapter Twenty-eight
Robert

Mel shifted in her chair, the one Robert had saved for her. This time she reached for his hand and got a squeeze and a wide grin. "Thanks for that. Are you okay?" he whispered in her ear. She nodded and squeezed back with more effort than usual. It felt good to give his support.

"You know," she whispered back to Robert, "he was a player, and I didn't know it."

She bowed her head and the tears started to stream. Robert took her hand and led her outside into the hallway. He wrapped his arms around her and let her soak his shirt. "Let it out, Mel, all out." He squeezed her closer to his chest and nuzzled her luxurious hair with his nose. Smelled so good. "A new perfume? It's citrusy, and I love it. So you." Well, that didn't help as he'd hoped. She choked and sobbed more. "Stay here while I go grab your purse. We are getting out of here." He turned on his heels, rushed back into the session as quietly as possible, grabbed her purse and thrust it in her hands. "Now, let's go."

The closest restaurant near the hospital where the grief sessions were held was IHOP. Always dependable, and he knew most of the servers since he dined alone so much. It would do. It had to.

"Hi, Rosemary. How are you this evening?"

"Well, hello, Mr. Robert." The server raised her eyebrows. "Table for two tonight?"

Melanie raised her eyebrows, too. He decided to answer the unasked question. "What? I told you I know most of the waitstaff. They even know what I order." Melanie blinked several times. He hoped the deluge wasn't going to start again. He shrugged. "Guess I come here way too much. Gotta try another place to eat, but this is convenient, and predictable."

Melanie swallowed the last bite of her pot roast. It was delicious, but she wasn't comfortable eating a senior, over fifty-five plus meal at half the price of the other options. She was almost certain Robert was in his thirties. So, what he was doing was a scam. The overly friendly waitress scooped up their plates. "Did you like your entrée, Ma'am? And you, Mr. Almost Senior, how was yours?" She winked.

"It was delish as usual." Robert and Trixie the waitress laughed. He paid the bill and they headed out to his car. Melanie steamed.

"I can't believe you did that."

"What?"

"Faked being fifty-five plus to get a cheaper meal. For both of us."

Robert pulled her close to him. "Melanie, you are so adorable, and," he added, "so clueless."

She tried to push away, but his strong arms held

her.

"But, you lied. You paid the senior price for each of our meals."

"Nope. Didn't."

"No?"

"Trixie and I have an agreement, and IHOP is flexible. Yes, I order the senior meal because I crave pot roast. But, Trixie puts it on the bill at full price. It isn't offered on the regular menu, unfortunately. So, this nice woman who I went to high school with figures it out to be fair." He held her at arm's length and looked closely into her face. "You okay with that? Was your dinner good?"

Melanie nodded. "I am so embarrassed I didn't trust you. Thanks for telling me. I feel like a fool." She lowered her quivering chin. "Yes, dinner was delicious. Yum."

~

Why was she such a stress case, especially about Larry's mother? The woman wasn't hanging out at her apartment tonight when she got home. But, she wondered where she was. Because she was worried about Francine, or worried about her own safety? Where did the woman go at night? Was she safe? Did she have food and shelter?

Melanie picked up Lola and held her close. The dog licked her chin and whined. She clicked the pink leash on the pink collar. Maybe a brisk walk would do them both good.

Did it really matter where Larry's mother, was tonight? Maybe, maybe not.

Chapter Twenty-nine
Transformation

Natalie closed the gym and decided to drive by Melanie's huge apartment complex. She loved sitting with Mel on the tiny veranda and sipping coffee while looking out over the calm water of the Back Bay and getting a glimpse of the tumultuous Pacific, though they couldn't see the waves crashing on the sand. Even in super hot weather being up so high gave them a slight breeze, enough to ruffle their hair. Lola usually laid between them on the tile with her back legs spread and her pointy snout between her front paws. It was a respite for all of them. Tonight they should probably have an iced drink to cool them off, maybe Honey Tea.

Nat rang the buzzer and rang again. No response. Maybe Mel was delayed at the preschool. She should have called. She decided to drive all the way around the road circling the apartments. Perhaps Mel and Lola were out for an early evening walk. Halfway around she spotted a heap on the sidewalk. Curiosity got to her. Maybe a pile of trash for the recycle day. No, they didn't have that in Newport since they paid a small monthly fee to have all garbage separated. Maybe a pile of clothes for Salvation Army to pick up, but no sign taped to it. Then, she saw it move. Just a bit, just enough.

Nat stopped her little car and flew out the driver's door forgetting to close it. She did remember to put it in park. She approached the barely moving lump with caution, then she heard the moan.

~

This time Melanie's door flew open with Nat's push. She gasped and gave Nat the 'why me' stare.

"Is this who I think it is?" Nat asked. Not waiting for a reply she said, "Found her half off the sidewalk onto the street. Other side of apartments. Maybe so you wouldn't see her?"

Together they managed to guide the bundle of woman onto the sofa where she immediately collapsed. Her clothes were filthy, so was what hair they could see under her grimy Bad Hair Day cap. She twisted her hands together, gnarled and dirty. A single gold band was on her left ring finger. Melanie had never noticed that before, not during the court proceedings or any of the other times she had come across Larry's mother. Had Francine married again? After leaving Larry's dad? Or was she clinging to her old vows?

"Sorry I smell. No bath, no toilet. Just sorry." The woman locked eyes for a second with Melanie and collapsed deeper into the sofa. Melanie looked at the brown face with tears making trails on it. She gestured to Nat and together the two of them hefted the woman toward the bathroom where they filled the tub with foamy, scented water, stripped off her layers of clothing and practically heaved her in before running from the bathroom.

"I don't know what to do," Mel whispered to Natalie. "She is not my responsibility."

"But," Nat replied, "she has a connection with you."

"Yeh, right. Larry the deceiver, and his long gone mother the other deceiver."

"What," Nat asked out of the blue, "does Robert think?"

"You're kidding, right? He is not part of this scenario, just a friend."

"But, probably good one. One who cares about you and your situation." Nat turned Melanie toward her, clasping her shoulders. "He is a therapist. Surely, he has some insight. And, he knows about this situation."

Melanie ran from the room. "Gotta check on the woman in the tub. Make sure she hasn't drowned."

Nat followed her and grabbed some clean towels on the shelf over the tub. When they let the tub water out they both stared. The dark-skinned woman was emaciated, almost like a skeleton. Skin hung from her fragile bones. Her formerly tangled hair dangled in limp strands. But, she was clean and smelled good. She gifted the two girls with a hollow laugh.

Francine cackled revealing big gaps in her teeth. "See that dirt, girls?" She pointed to the once white tub, now with brown sides and bottom. "That's what I been livin' in."

Both women covered their mouths. "That's right girls, hold your pretty noses," she sneered. "Too bad that fancy bath didn't rub the color off my skin. You woulda liked that, huh?"

Melanie recovered first, maybe because she had

dealt with Francine before. Or, maybe because there was a connection. She really hadn't wanted one, but if Larry were alive she was bound to have met the woman sometime. "I'll go get the big scrub brush," she announced while shoving Francine onto the toilet lid and draping a towel over her shoulders. "You," she pointed to Nat, "get this woman some clothes from my closet. A robe or caftan, maybe. NOT my blue skirt."

"Coward," Nat sniggered. She grabbed one gnarled brown hand and tugged. "Let's go, lady."

"Hah. I ain't no lady, missy. But, I ain't gonna argue. I like the title. 'Specially if I'm gonna wear a real lady's clothes."

Nat dug through Mel's closet shoving her prettiest things aside. May as well get something the woman could wear outside since she figured that's where they were going to send her. It was getting hot, close to summer heat, so she looked for light weight items. But, if the woman did end up sleeping under a bridge, or wherever she lodged, she would get cold at night. Nat found a long-sleeved tee in a hideous green. She had always hated that on Melanie, so she tossed it to Francine who now perched on the edge of the bed. Next was a pair of ancient bell-bottom pants. Why had Mel hung onto them? She had never been the hippy type. She rummaged through a drawer and found all-cotton undies that Mel probably used for gym wear. And a workout bra way too big for skinny Francine, but it would have to do. She found a big safety pin and tucked some of the back fabric in with it.

The little black woman was rapidly pulling on clothes as if they might disappear. Everything hung on her small frame, but she seemed to relish each item. She clapped her hands and twirled. "Fresh! Smells so good. Soft." Nat almost cried.

Nat and Mel took so much for granted. Clean clothes, soft fabrics, pretty colors. She was almost sorry the pants she gave Francine were black. But, maybe best if she slept on the ground.

Mel came in the room dripping with sweat from scrubbing the tub. She gasped looking at Francine. "You gave her my old Eileen Fisher pants?"

"Mel, they are terribly outdated. Bell bottoms. You were saving those?"

"Uh, sort of. I save all of that designer's old clothes to turn them in for discounts when I buy something new. It's called "Give us back our clothes." But, I would only have gotten five dollars for them." She rolled her eyes and sighed. "No matter. It's fine. My blue skirt still in the closet?"

Nat nodded. She knew her eyes were glistening. "Shoes? Something for her feet?" The two women looked down at Francine's feet. Clean now, but with ugly long toenails. And, they were so tiny. Mel's size sevens would fall right off.

"Got to do the right thing," Nat said with conviction. "Can't take her to a salon, but we can do it ourselves."

Two hours later the old woman had an amateur manicure and pedicure, by novices. Her short cut nails were painted with a clear polish, and her toes with a pale pink. They had trimmed and styled her minimal hair tufts thankful no lice were on her scalp as they had expected. The only part of her left to revise was her mouth, her teeth to be exact.

"Not much we can do about them," Nat said.

"Unless you have relative who's a dentist. A kind, compassionate one," she chuckled. Nat could almost see the wheels turning in Mel's head. She raised her brows. "Yes? Idea?"

Mel shook her head. "Not for now."

"Hungry."

Nat and Mel looked at each other, both women's cheeks crimson with embarrassment. "How could we have forgotten?" Mel said.

"Too focused on filth." Nat raced to the tiny laundry room with the pile of Francine's dirty clothes.

"No. Stop, Nat. Just toss them. Please." Mel waved her arms in front of her face. "I'm sorry to sound like a prude, but I don't want them in my washing machine. K?" She held out a large black trash bag for Nat to dump the items in. After taking it out to the trash can in her apartment garage, they both scrubbed their hands – a lot.

"Hungry."

Was there an echo in the kitchen?

"Eggs," Mel said mater of factly. "Cheese, milk, and," she hesitated, "bacon. Do I have any?"

"You do. But, you also have a flank steak marinating in a plastic bag. Big enough for a few."

Melanie slapped her forehead. "I almost forgot. That's for tonight, for Robert, for dinner."

"Guess that's out then. Eggs will be fine. What time is he supposed to come?" She took out the carton of eggs, cracked a few and started to scramble them in the first pan she grabbed.

"You are way too efficient, Nat."

"Gotta be when you own a gym. Have to open on time, close on time and keep all equipment clean.

Business does that to you." She smiled.

"I would love to own a business. I love teaching the adorable kids, but it would be so nice to be my totally own boss."

"What is your dream? Do you want to have your own preschool? I'm sure it's something to do with children." Nat pushed the eggs in the skillet while she talked. The bacon was frying, and Mel had put bread in the toaster.

"Sort of. My dream is to have a children's book store. Filled with inspirational, mostly Christian, kids' books. I think there is a need for that."

"Hungry."

"Coming soon," Mel said, then made a face at Nat. "What are we going to do? With her I mean."

Nat stopped stirring and crossed her arms over her chest. "There must be a women's shelter we can take her to."

"But, none close. They are all mostly in Santa Ana. And, it's late. It would take too long to drive her there, enroll her and come back in time for my dinner with Robert."

"Yeh. And they'd ask a lot of questions about your relationship to her. I don't know what to advise you. It's a sticky situation. Sorry I brought her in."

"It's okay. I'm sure God had all that arranged. Now, if He'd just tell me how to go forward."

~

The old woman scarfed down her food like a hungry jackal that had just caught its prey. After several burps and holding her belly, she hobbled to the sofa and collapsed. Mel covered her with an afghan and put a tissue near her mouth where the drool was dripping.

What was she to do with her almost mother-in-law? What does God want her to do? She prayed hard He would guide her. She needed His wisdom now. Now, God, please, now.

"You take her, Nat. Please just for tonight until I can get things sorted out."

"I know you feel desperate, friend, but I can't. My digs are so small I can hardly fit in them. Remember when Larry came to visit me. Before you and he fell in love?" Nat lowered her eyes at both the memory and her friend's reaction. Had she been too insensitive? She got the courage to press on. "He bunked with Bill Lord when Vivian was in Scottsdale helping Connie with her pregnancy issues." She felt pin prickles on her skin. "Hey! That's the answer. The Lords have that extra room they say is always open for company. I bet they would take her, at least for tonight. And, Vivian will lavish love on her." She pulled her phone from her purse pocket and hit a button.

Chapter Thirty
Vivian

The woman standing before her was shaking like the proverbial leaf. It was warm out tonight, so Vivian knew her tremors weren't from cold. Had to be fear. She remembered shaking like that the night Bill had asked to meet her at Starbucks, the night he told her he loved her. But, she hadn't had a clue what the meeting was about. She had thought it was about her daughter Candy and her indecision about marrying Will her AA husband again. Boy, was she wrong. God had mysterious ways to bring people together.

Vivian threw her arms around the slight frame of a woman and practically dragged her into the foyer. Natalie stood behind looking baffled. "I . . . I didn't mean to impose, Viv. Mel and I just need a respite."

"Of course you do, sweet girl. So does this woman. Let me take care." She smiled at Nat and blinked. "Now scoot."

The shaking finally stopped, probably from Vivian's strong arms squeezing tight. Natalie had explained on the phone about the entire situation, including the scenario of the bathtub. But, mostly the link between Melanie and Francine. Although Vivian already knew, she was ready. She knew about the relationship, and she knew the drill. She knew Mel and Nat almost as children of her own. She knew how to take care of desperate people. That was her role, a nurturer. She could do this. She loved doing this.

Bill stood behind her glaring. "What, who, are we taking in now?" he said. Vivian knew that tone. But, when she had been away helping Connie, he took Larry in without reservation. She glared back.

"This is my calling, Bill. You knew that when we married," Vivian lowered her chin and scowled at him. He shrugged and stomped out of the room.

She put the tiny woman to bed in the guest room and tucked her in under the snowy white comforter. The little woman started to weep, and her hands became restless, flopping all over the place. "I never," she whispered between tears.

"You never what, dear?" Vivian asked kindly.

"Nobody never cared. I can't remember when I had a soft bed and clean sheets." She swiped her eyes with gnarled hands and turned her cheek into the soft pillow.

"Sleep tonight, dear one. Tomorrow we will talk." Vivian tucked the sheets around the little emaciated brown frame, squeezed a fragile hand and kissed her on the forehead. Before she closed the door of the bedroom, she prayed. "Guidance, Lord. I need guidance. And discernment. I don't know why I feel so conflicted, but I do know You sent her to me. I want to do Your will." She pulled the door shut quietly and heard it click. A cup of tea begged her, so she went to the kitchen and made one.

"Do I hear the kettle boiling?" Bill sauntered into the room like nothing new had happened. Vivian bit her tongue. She knew he wasn't really clueless, but why did men like to act that way? Her son Billy did the same thing. So had Will her son-in-law. Like, "What's going on?" Men!

He knew perfectly well what was going on. Bill had actually been there when Natalie brought the little woman.

"So, who is she, and why do we have her?" Bill's anger laced his words.

"Do you really care?"

He lowered his head. "Yeh. Guess it's important to Melanie, and Nat. You know I care about them."

"You do remember Larry, I assume?"

"Nice guy. Stayed here when you were in Scottsdale. Ostensibly taking care of Connie."

"Stop right there, Bill. I went there to help Connie with a difficult pregnancy. I had no idea her sister was coming, too. But, it all worked out. I *was* needed and grateful for it." Vivian shook her head at the memories. "I'm glad I went. It was also a gift to me." She poked him in the chest, lightly. "Do you understand?"

He nodded. "I forgive you. Now, tell me about this woman."

"YOU forgive me?" Her voice carried across the kitchen and made the overhead fan wobble. She stomped from the room carrying her tea cup. He could fill his own.

~

"What happened, God, to the strong man I married?" Vivian perched on the side of their bed, their marriage bed. She felt so alone, and confused. Bill was the prime member of the group who arranged donations to struggling entrepreneurs. He was the boss, so to speak, of the small group who provided financial hope. She knew he and the secret group had done that for Connie. Now, thanks to them, Connie and Jaeda had a thriving couture business. And, because of it, Doreen had a major modeling career. Blessings passed down.

Melanie, nor Natalie, had asked nothing of him or the group. They only asked for the little brown woman to be taken in. Vivian knew there was more, but what?

She knew the history, knew Francine (was that really her name?) would have become Melanie's mother-in-law if the marriage between her and Larry had lasted, if he hadn't died in prison. What she didn't know was why. Why had the woman suddenly appeared after over thirty years, the woman who had abandoned Larry and his dad when the boy was a toddler? She decided the why was not her concern. God knew the why, and He had sent the woman to her. She would take care of her and find out the why. God will answer. She remembered Habakkuk 2:3. The reason would be revealed in time and "it will certainly come." She put down her cup of tea and returned to the kitchen. Bill was still there sipping from his cup. She put her arms around him. They were back again.

Chapter Thirty-one
Court Again

Melanie felt guilty. She and Natalie had foisted Francine off on Vivian. Still, the mother of all mothers, as Vivian liked to call herself, accepted the hand-off gracefully. She had even seemed excited from what Nat told her. Melanie wished she could be as excited about taking care of Francine. What, she wondered, did God have in mind placing the woman in her life? How would Larry have felt if he had lived? Would he accept his mother back after over thirty years?

She wished she could go to his grave and ask him. But, his grave was in Arizona, and she was in California. Maybe she should take a quick trip there. Kneeling at his grave would give her comfort. That's when she got the call.

"Scottsdale Police. Are you Melanie Carson Langston? We have some new information about your deceased husband. Can you come to the precinct at eight tomorrow morning?"

She explained she lived in California. "Oh, how about Saturday?"

She could do that but requested more reason to come. The officer on the other end of the phone said he couldn't say, but her presence was important. She called Randi her attorney friend.

"Not sure why you are still calling me, girl. What's wrong?"

Melanie tried to explain, but she wasn't sure either. "Any way you can figure it out? I sure don't want to fly to Arizona for nothing."

"Let me look up everything I can find on Larry, his internment and death."

Melanie heard alternating silence and clicking. Computer keys? She grabbed a soda out of the fridge and lowered herself on the worn couch. Picking at the tatty binding of the pillows, she wondered why she had never replaced the old monster. She had enough money saved. She could run on a Saturday morning and go to IKEA and have one delivered by Tuesday. Was it because she had hoped for her and Larry to make a permanent home? Not sure about anything now, she heard Randi's voice back on the phone.

"I found something, Mel." Randi's voice sounded weird. Skeptical? "It could be good or iffy. Not necessarily bad, just a possibility. A slim one."

~

Melanie boarded the early flight from John Wayne Airport in Orange County to fly to Phoenix. She still wasn't a hundred percent sure why she was going. Even Randi said it was a pie in the sky. Maybe a waste of money and time. Randi wasn't comfortable as an attorney on collective class actions suits. So many were scams enticing people to join and get a pittance for some minor disturbance. So many got only a few dollars, or maybe if lucky, a few hundred.

When she met the two attorneys who were presenting the class action suit, she was not impressed. Both men wore wrinkled suits in some kind of sleazy fabric. Not professional like Randi. Still, they smiled and gave encouraging words. What else could she ask?

They stood outside a courtroom in Phoenix with a small group of other people. She tried to look anonymous, but a few others kept squeezing her shoulder and delivering wan smiles.

A bosomy woman with dark hair and a warm smile who spoke in broken English attached herself to Melanie and asked about "Your guy? He dies in prison, too?"

Mel nodded and gave a bleak smile back. "Yours sick?" the woman asked.

Mel nodded again. "Bad care. Bad medical. My son die," she went on, "of flu bug." She rolled her eyes toward the ceiling. "How that happen? Bad doctors?" She finally let go of Mel's shoulder and walked away to join a group speaking in Spanish. Mostly women, all weeping and hugging each other. Mel wished she had someone to hug her.

Why hadn't she asked Natalie to come with her? She still didn't understand why she was there. Because Larry died in prison of the flu? Hadn't he had good care from prison doctors? She'd never questioned it. She'd trusted. Looking around the group of people gathered in the hallway, she wondered why she had. They hadn't. Why had she?

Randi had told her it was very unusual for plaintiffs in a class action suit to even appear in court. Mostly, it was handled by a group of attorneys (Mel had heard the snicker in Randi's voice) who presented the case to the judge. Still, she had been called to come, and she was anxious to learn and experience the proceedings. The door of the courtroom clicked open, and they all filed in.

Chapter Thirty-two
Thief?

"What does this mean, Randi?" Melanie held the phone close to her ear to block out the background noise. People were cheering, mostly in a language she didn't understand. Maybe living in California it was time to take Spanish lessons. She had waited for Randi's response having been told by the receptionist she was with a client. When Randi finally came on Mel heard laughter.

"What's so funny? Did I win or lose?"

"You," Randi said with a chuckle, "you and a bunch of other people won. That's what class action suits do."

"Oh, how much?"

"Not much in the scheme of things. But enough to pay for his burial. 'Course, you already did that."

"How did this happen? I don't understand."

"The state of Arizona has been under fire for several years for not giving good medical care to prisoners. Larry died at just the right time." Mel could hear Randi taking a deep breath. "Sorry. Bad comment,

very unprofessional, very unfriendly. Sorry, girl."
Melanie could almost see Randi holding her head.

"Forget it. I forgive. I might have said the same
thing myself."

"When you get back to Newport with all the
paperwork, I will go over it with you. One thing I'm
almost sure of is you will not get a large amount from
this class action suit. But, maybe enough, as I said, to
pay some burial bills."

"That's okay. I never expected anything. But, if I
do get something I want to give it to his mom."

Randi said, "We will talk," and put down the
phone.

Melanie called Natalie next, but got a voicemail.
She didn't want to go into a long explanation and knew
it, so she simply said, "I won" and knew there would be
a zillion questions. She would leave that for when she
returned to California.

Vivian picked up on the second ring, obviously
jostling with Bill. "I've got it!"

"No, Bill, it's Mel calling . . . for me," she
emphasized the pronoun. Mel could visualize her raised
brows and clamped lips. Those two, they bantered back
and forth all the time, but they seemed to love it, and
love each other. Maybe second marriages between
widowed spouses did that. She raised her own brows
and chuckled beneath her breath.

"Hello, Mel dear. She's fine, doing great. I
presume you called about your mother-in-law."

"I don't really like to call her that, Vivian, but yes,
about Francine. I hope she hasn't been too much
trouble."

"Trouble? Hah. She's been a delight to take care

of. Such a gentle soul, and so grateful."

Melanie hadn't told Vivian about Francine's un-gentle times, especially the one when she broke into Mel's apartment and ransacked her kitchen, throwing food all over the room. Not a good memory. Suddenly, she got a brain flash, but she was reluctant to worry Vivian. She knew Bill would go ballistic if she asked the question of him. So, she approached it delicately with Vivian.

"Uh, remember, Vivian, she's been homeless for a long time. She also desperately wanted the ring Larry gave to me. Not for sentimental reasons, but for its value." She paused and measured her next words. "I," she cleared her throat, "worry she might be tempted to rummage through drawers, maybe even take a piece of jewelry or silverware." She heard a harrumph on the other end but steeled herself to press on. Vivian had to know, had to protect her belongings. With great courage she asked "Vivian. Are your valuables locked up? Like in a safe, or at the bank?"

Silence.

The gap in conversation worried Melanie. Was Vivian remembering something?

"Well," the older woman said almost in a whisper. "I don't want Bill to know this, but I can't find a broach he gave me. Not all that valuable, just costume, but it was his mother's." Sigh. "You don't really think . . . do you?"

"Sadly, I do. At least it's a possibility. I hate to say this, but I think you should check for anything of any value, whether costume or real, if it's important to you." She almost added, "Or to Bill." But Vivian would have to deal with her husband. Not Melanie's responsibility.

Bill was a dear man, a very rich man by most standards. As an entrepreneur he had made a lot of money, mostly from investments. At least that's what Mel had been told the one time she had sort of dated Candy's brother Billy, Vivian's only son. The mini-grapevine in Newport credited Big Bill, as many called him, and a secret group of men with donating start-up monies to young entrepreneurs. But, nothing was ever confirmed. That's how secret it was. She'd often wondered if Connie had been one of them and had started her design studio that way. As close as the Candy Canes were, she would never know because she'd heard the one codicil the recipients had to swear to, even signing legal papers, was to never reveal how they got the funds, nor from whom. Actually, she'd heard, they didn't even know for sure. The second thing they had to promise was to give back, to help others after they became successful. She remembered reading in the local paper that Winning Designs donated a large sum to the neo-natal unit at Honor Health Hospital in Arizona where Connie and Jaeda's twins were born. Maybe that was just being grateful their babies were healthy.

She heard silence again. Where was Vivian?

A rustling sound alerted her. "Vivian?"

Chapter Thirty-three
Reflection

Melanie thought she would throw up. How could Natalie have convinced her to thrust the old woman on Vivian? The old woman was obviously a thief. Vivian's most precious belongings were missing. She could imagine how a few small items of jewelry could be concealed, but twelve sterling silver fish forks from Sweden? Those couldn't possibly be hidden on that slight body. Then she remembered the gray satchel the woman kept close to her, the one never opened.

"I don't believe it," Nat said with certainty. "Sorry, I don't see how she could do that, nor why." Another silence, this time from Mel. She thought her heart would break. How could she have made this mistake to trust Larry's mother? The mother who had abandoned him when he was only a toddler, the mother who had never tried to contact him for over thirty years. How could she, Melanie, have been so wrong? Natalie, too.

They were stretched on chaises on Melanie's patio overlooking the Back Bay shrouded with evening mist. The minute view of the Pacific disappeared in the dark before they could speak. So much for the ocean view the apartment complex touted in its ads. The lounge chairs squeaked when Nat crossed her ankles. "You sound like a mating duck," Mel laughed. "At least you don't quack."

Lola jumped on Melanie and emitted a sound somewhat like a duck. Her whine varied in resonance from a whimper to an almost bark. She tried so hard, but the horrible former owner who had her voice box surgically removed left her without a real doggie bark. Dr. Price, Mel's veterinarian, said he would never do that, never. Still, it had been done, and sweet Lola nuzzled her long snout under Melanie's chin. Melanie ran her fingers through the wispy white topknot and the dog settled with a sigh onto her legs.

"I don't know what to think, Nat. She is a desperate woman. It's a sad situation, and I feel responsible for shoving her off on Vivian."

"But," Nat turned in the squeaky metal chaise to focus on Melanie, "Vivian loves to do rescuing. It's kind of her mission in life. She could have said no."

"But, it didn't have to be us, me, to ask her. I feel so guilty. We knew Francine was a derelict, not a stable person. If I hadn't had to rush off to Arizona to be at that hearing, I could have taken care of her here. Oh, why did I do that to Vivian? What can I do to make amends?"

"Well," Nat seemed to be collecting her thoughts. "You can take her back, take care of her, or put her somewhere."

"Like?"

"There must be some kind of county or state home, somewhere they take indigent people."

Melanie glared at her. "What are you suggesting? She's homeless."

"Not really anymore. She has a definite connection, actually two, with you as her daughter-in-law and Vivian. Bill, too. I think you might have some legal responsibility. Ask Randi."

~

"What? You want to take full legal responsibility for her? Melanie, are you crazy?" Randi slapped her forehead. Not very lawyer-like, but Melanie realized her friend was frustrated. Besides, she didn't have to always have a bland face and appear stoic. "Do you even have a clue what this could involve?"

Melanie shrugged.

"I will need to research this, but I'm very much against it. Both as an attorney and your friend. I think you are placing yourself into a quagmire. A legal one and an emotional one." Randi sat back in her ergonomic chair and tapped a red fingernail on the papers in front of her. "It sounds to me as if you want to adopt her. And, if you do take custody of her, she's yours for the rest of your life." Randi clasped her hands together and rested them under her chin. Melanie noticed her knuckles were turning white.

Melanie shrugged again, but this time wrapped her almost numb arms around her chest. Randi wouldn't let up.

"Can she swim?"

"What?"

"Can she swim?" Randi's eyes lit up almost glittering in the fluorescent overhead lights, and there was a tremor around her barely smiling lips. Like she was trying to contain her laughter.

"What are you talking about? You are making no sense. Who cares if she can swim?"

"This is off the wall, out of the box, crazy, but . . ." She put picked up a pen and started to scribble on a yellow Post-it. "Don't know if this has ever been done before, but worth exploring."

"I . . . I don't understand. What are you getting at?"

Randi put the pen down with a slam and looked into Melanie's face, straight on. "The Candy Canes." Mel felt her face blanche. What was Randi suggesting? She, Melanie, had been accepted in the special group after proving she could swim ten laps. A few had seemed skeptical, but all had finally embraced her. She had never let them down, was always there for each and every one of them in prayer and support. What was Randi implying?

Chapter Thirty-four
Decisions

"What? What? What?" Melanie knew it wasn't a genuine echo, but it sounded like one. More questions came to barrage her. Natalie was laughing so hard and flopped on Mel's sofa that she was holding her stomach, and tears plastered her face. Fortunately, she seldom wore makeup as the owner of Nat's Gym who led classes. No mascara running or smudged lip gloss.

"You are crazy." Nat choked out the words between laughs.

"I am, aren't I? But, in my defense it was Randi's idea. Actually, a doable one, one we could collectively do." She sighed. "But, we would all have to agree."

Candy on the group phone call spoke the first intelligible words. Her voice was laced with anger. "Mel, you have already foisted this woman on my mother and Bill. How can you even consider asking us to do more?"

Connie interjected. Her voice was soft, Connie soft. "We need to learn more, and we need to embrace Mel and her almost mother-in-law. We should be compassionate, not judgmental."

Jaeda grabbed the phone from Connie. "I agree. After what we've been through with Connie's pregnancy and how God blessed us, it's time for us to bless others."

Doreen spoke next, but her voice quavered. "I will do whatever you need, Mel. Connie gave me a whole new life. It's about time I give one to someone else. I'm in."

Cindy's voice sounded hollow coming all the way from Costa Rica. Mel had always thought of her as the super sensitive one and the one who made common sense out of unusual situations. Maybe the one most connected to God. Mel thought about how Cindy and Rob were sent to the lonely Central American beach town to bring souls to Christ by planting a church. Maybe this was where she should send her small procurement from the class action suit. Was God nudging her to do that?

"Hi, sweet Cindy. Any thoughts?" Mel hoped she would bring all of them together. It was a huge hope.

"I do," Cindy said with a clear, calm voice. "First, we must pray about this, and pray for the woman whose future may be in our hands."

Mel was blown away. Cindy always seemed to have the perfect perspective. No anger, no asking about Francine's faith. Just a simple way to approach the situation, prayer. Then, she asked, "Where is Noelle? Is she on the line?"

Several voices yelled, "Noelle, are you there?" Silence. Mel checked her phone and saw the group line had alerted Noelle. Where was she? "Should we start to worry?"

Cindy centered them all. "God says to not worry. It's an emotion lost in today. We must focus on tomorrow because it will have worries of its own."

Mel couldn't imagine with Cindy's faith why she and Rob hadn't established a flourishing church in that little beach area outside of Jaco, Costa Rica. God must have a reason for their waiting time, and their years of patience. Then, she remembered the verse in Habakkuk 2:3 where God says it will come just at the right time. She silently prayed for that for Cindy and Rob, God's angels.

Noelle finally came on. "Sorry, gals, having Braxton Hicks."

They all gasped. "Are you all right?"

"Okay now, thanks. But, I have been listening to your conversations. I do have a thought." They heard the hesitation in her voice. She took a deep breath. "Mel, everyone, this woman is not a project. She is a woman. A project is something assigned, like I assign projects in my classes. For a grade, for a reward. Francine should be our reward, not an assignment."

~

"Why, why, haven't I involved Vivian in this conversation, this decision?" Mel's chin was resting on her neck and her words were barely a whisper. She looked to Natalie sitting next to her on the sofa.

"Because," Nat said, "you wanted to do it all on your own, make your own decision. I know you called all the Candy Canes and asked, but you wanted the ultimate outcome to be yours. Your decision." She winked at Melanie. "*'Miss I am in control Mel.'*"

Mel almost put the phone down. She was discouraged, hopeless. Then, Cindy spoke.

"We are all in, Mel, but we have one request, that you bring Vivian and Bill into the final decision."

Chapter Thirty-five
Vivian

"Hmph. What's up with you girls?" Bill's gruff voice startled them all. He sounded angry. Melanie hoped he was just frustrated. The man liked to eat, and right now his dinner was probably on hold. She heard the passing of the phone and the grumpy and sassy interchange.

"For you."

"Maybe for both of us, Mr. Know it All."

Vivian put the phone on speaker mode. Melanie wasn't sure that was a great idea when all the girls could hear the couples' bantering. But, the choice wasn't theirs.

"Girls," Vivian squealed, "are you all there?" Melanie was sure several heads automatically nodded, but she spoke for all of them.

"Yes, Vivian, we are all here." She had expected Vivian to complain about Francine, but what she heard was very different. When Vivian spoke, Melanie reached for Natalie's hand.

"I have exciting news, girls. Are you all sitting down?" Vivian had always been a bit dramatic. So, Mel steeled herself for the announcement. She was sure the others had too.

"Francine is recovered, whole, healthy, safe and . . ." Why was she dragging this out?

"Girls, she has accepted our Lord!"

Melanie wanted to be sure she'd heard it right. "What? You're kidding, or at least trying to encourage us."

"Nope. God's honest promise."

"How? What did you do?"

"Nothing. God did it all. Trust me, please."

"But, how? How did He do it? This is big, Vivian. Big."

"This will sound crazy, but here is what happened." Melanie held the phone away from her ear, but she heard Vivian's words.

"He," Vivian emphasized He, God, "sent a messenger to our door."

"Don't include me in this, Viv." Mel could hear Bill's voice in the background.

Mel and the others knew Bill Lord to be a strong Christian man, so why did he sound so dubious? Was Vivian making a big deal out of a small incident?

More bantering. "Bill, stop! You know what you saw, you were there, you answered the door. Why are you being unbelieving?" Mel thought she heard an "ow." Did Vivian punch Bill in the arm?

"Sorry, girls, but what happened is true. Let me tell you . . . in detail."

Melanie could feel the tension on the multiple phone lines. She felt it herself gripping her phone so tightly her palm was sweating. Vivian might be a bit dramatic, but she was sincere and honest. A woman of

faith. She waited for Vivian to begin.
"The stage is all yours, Vivian."

Chapter Thirty-six
The Package

The chuckle on the other end was so Vivian, setting up for her announcement. Finally, they heard a whooshing breath. "Okay, girls, hang onto your hats. You especially, Melanie."

Melanie snickered at the ancient phrase. Susan her mother often used it, a throwback from World War II when her mother was a child. Women wore hats in those days, but she never knew why they had to hang on to them. She did know women in England wore them for every occasion. Protocol. A bow to royalty? She brought herself back from her skittering thoughts.

Vivian was talking.

"I'm sure you've heard the phrase that God's specialty is recovering the lost." She waited for murmurs of confirmation, then continued. Mel could almost see her nodding her head and smiling. What had made Vivian so sure about Francine accepting Christ?

One thing about Vivian, Mel thought, is she doesn't drone on. She gets right to the heart of the matter.

"It all started when the doorbell rang." Well, maybe she did.

"I hesitated because it was almost seven. Still, Amazon delivers until eight, but we hadn't ordered anything recently. I opened the shutters and peeked out the side window. He wasn't in a uniform, but Amazon delivery people seldom are nowadays. He wore a pink button-down shirt – pink! Khaki pants and a grin. He was about fifty-five plus and dark chocolate. I liked his smile, trusted it."

Maybe Vivian does drone on. Still, it was her stage.

"I opened the door and invited him in. I admit I thought seeing someone of her own color might cheer Francine. What I hadn't noticed was the leash attached to his arm. He had a dog!"

"You sure, Ma'am? Can Sam come in, too?"

"That's when Bill got on his high horse."

'No dogs! No dogs in here. I am allergic.'

"Phew, Bill, I said. Get over it. I let the man and the dog inside." Vivian paused for a breath, but as Mel expected, she continued in an instant.

"Carlos was a nice man, a gentle soul. He appropriately removed his cap and held Sam the dog close, then held out an envelope, actually a small package."

'For a Francine?' He looked at the package again, then looked up confused. 'No last name. Maybe I got the wrong place.'

"I gestured to her. She was sitting in Bill's recliner, hands folded across her chest. She waved a hand in the air and smiled. 'That's me,' she said. 'Francine no name.'"

Mel could almost see Bill screwing up his face. "Bill was fuming," Vivian said, but Mel heard a chuckle under her breath. What a team.

'I said no dogs in here!'

"Bill, I said, cool it. The man has the little, did you notice little, dog under his arms. Covered by his sleeve, so no dog hair floating around the house."

Mel decided Vivian was a master at diffusing uncomfortable situations. She recalled so many times when Vivian stifled others' negative comments or actions to center everyone and bring them back to reason.

"Shush, Bill. Let me continue with my story." A door slammed, but Vivian didn't sound as if she noticed.

"The man walked in holding the little dog, bowed in front of Francine as if she was royalty, held out the package, then waited for her to open it. He didn't move."

BONNIE ENGSTROM

Chapter Thirty-seven
Questions

"This can't be real."

Melanie whispered into the cool evening breeze blowing off the Back Bay and the turbulent Pacific a few miles away. She loved the ocean and often wished she could afford to live closer to the sound of the waves. But, living closer meant being a millionaire who could afford a massive house perched overlooking the foam. She was content, even happy and blessed, with her life. She had a job nurturing precious little ones and a passel of friends. Still, she had her new mother-in-law, regretfully. What had Larry saddled her with? Was he looking down from heaven and laughing?

Vivian had assured her, she almost saw the woman crossing her heart, that Carlos was the key, the one sent from the Lord. She certainly hoped he was, because she was so over Francine.

"What can't be real?" Natalie asked. "You don't believe this could have happened?"

"Maybe my faith isn't as strong as yours, or certainly as Vivian's. It seems so strange. That's all."

"Maybe you should visit Francine. Ask. What made the difference? She is the one to reassure you, maybe to lead you back to your faith."

Chapter Thirty-eight
Visit

Melanie pushed the bell twice. She should have called. But it took a lot of courage for her to come.

Bill answered the door, almost ripping it off its hinges. "What? What do you want?" When he saw Melanie he rubbed his brow. "Sorry, Mel. You know you are always welcome. Just a stressful few days." He touched her hand and gestured her in.

The first thing she noticed was the dog smell. Then, before settling on the sofa she had to brush it off. Yep, dog hairs.

"I came here to see Francine." She didn't know what else to say.

"Of course. Let me get her." She heard some muttering under Bill's breath, but she couldn't decipher what the words were. Not happy words. She figured that out just before Francine bounced in.

"Hi, Sweetie. You came to see me?"

"Yes, I did. I want to know how you are doing, and," she hesitated, "anything new?"

"Can't you see the glow?" Francine twirled and

extended her fragile arms. The smile on her face said a zillion words. "I am a new woman, a woman loved and revered. I am a woman loved by God." She clutched the hem of her caftan, one Melanie was sure Vivian had lent her, and spun some more, then added, "And, a man."

All Melanie could get out of her mouth was, "Oh."

"That's all you can say, girl?" Francine leaned forward and stuck her nose in Melanie's face. "Whew. I thought you'd be pleased."

Chapter Thirty-nine

Answers

"I didn't know what to say." Melanie rubbed her eyes. Everything was blurry. Maybe because of the tears that hadn't escaped. They finally came in a deluge, and she started choking. Candy slapped her on the back, hard, and Mel sputtered.

She wasn't sure why Candy was here and not Natalie. Was she such a basket case the girls were taking turns? She turned to her friend admiring the long russet wavy hair cascading over her slim shoulders. "Why you, Can? Did you lose out on the Candy Cane lottery?"

Candy laughed her melodic deep laugh that resonated. Even throughout Mel's apartment making the bell ring. Or, was that really the bell?

"I'll get that. You expecting someone?" She turned to Melanie. "I wanted to come. Especially since it was my parents who took in Francine." She shook her head. "No, that's wrong. I really wanted to come. I love you and want to do anything I can to help you through this situation."

"But, it's all my fault, Larry's too. If we hadn't married, there would be no Francine."

"Oh, girl, wrong. There will always be Francines. You just inherited one." Candy swept past her to open the door.

The man standing before her was moderately handsome with graying hair and a smile that threatened to take over his face if he'd let it. Candy noticed he wore a blue shirt with the sleeves rolled up, the latest macho male thing, and khaki pants neatly pressed with a crease up the legs.

"Who are you?"

"Uh, Robert, Mel's friend." His warm smile finally exploded on his face and showed nice white teeth in a reassuring grin above a neat gray moustache. Candy grinned back. Mel had mentioned Robert. Hadn't he been a support to her in the grief group? She reached for his hand and pulled him in.

"I think she will be very glad to see you, Robert, and I think she needs you."

~

Robert was a bit taken back by the beautiful woman. Was she one of the special group? Must be he concluded in a millisecond. He fingered the collar of his shirt and adjusted his pants, making sure the belt was just right. He had been trying to get over these annoying gestures, so why was he doing them now? Especially when Melanie needed him. This was about her, not him.

He followed the Candy woman past the kitchen and onto the lanai where Melanie was hunched over on a chaise. His first thought was could she be sick? Then, he noticed her shoulders shaking. The girl was upset, distraught, sad.

I am a therapist who helps other people in their pain, and I don't know what to do.

BONNIE ENGSTROM

Chapter Forty
Uncertainty

"Is this really where you want me, Lord?" Robert whispered the words under his breath to himself. He knew he was falling in love with Melanie, but was it the right timing, even God's plan for them? She was still so fragile from her aborted marriage to Larry. Should he approach her to share his love for her? Or, should he wait? What, he asked the Almighty, is your timing?

Robert shuffled his feet on the worn carpet to make sure he was centered. He counted his steps approaching Melanie. When he reached her, he hesitated. Wanting to lift her into his arms he instead wiped his palm on his pant leg and placed a tentative hand on her shaking shoulder. Would his touch be enough?

Melanie felt his presence. "Robert, what are you doing here?"

"Just wanted to be." That was all he could say. Would his words be enough?

Not moving from the chaise chair, she reached a hand toward him without turning. "Thank you," was all she said.

Robert felt uncomfortable. Had he done the right thing? His feelings for Melanie were escalating. But, they confused him. Yes, it had been almost four sad years since his wife of ten years had died. He still hadn't accepted someone so young could die from cervical cancer, someone who had never born children, didn't even have the chance to. So often he asked what was God thinking? That's when he often picked up his Bible and turned to Isaiah 55. Verses 8-9 were what he called fall back verses. Reassuring and a reminder of whom was in control. He was thankful he had committed them to memory. Right now they were the only comfort he had.

"For my thoughts are not your thoughts, neither are your ways my ways," declares the LORD. "As the heavens are higher than the earth, so are my ways higher than your ways and my thoughts than your thoughts."

~

He rubbed the steering wheel of his car and wiped it off with the baby wipes he kept in the console. Putting it in park, he pulled his key out of the ignition slot and wiped it, too. After exiting and closing the driver's door he finally pocketed the key. So much for that. Done.

Holding the end of his sleeve to open the door to his trailer, what he hoped would only be his temporary home, he entered and sighed. It was okay now, no germs. But, he still had to fix dinner and pull the microwave box out of the freezer. Since it was icy cold, it was probably okay and would sanitize his fingers anyway. The microwave oven binged after three minutes. Now, with potholders, he could sit and eat after he wiped his fork with alcohol.

The food surprised him. It was delicious, and just enough to fill his stomach. Dapping at his mouth several times, he placed the container in the trash. Maybe he should call Melanie and apologize for leaving so abruptly. He wiped off his cellphone and dialed.

BONNIE ENGSTROM

Chapter Forty-one
Decisions

Melanie turned to Natalie with a questioning stare. "What do you think about Robert?"

"Ah, nice guy. Likes you a lot. Why are you asking?"

"Not sure. But he has a lot of strange gestures, seems odd."

"Like what?"

"He wipes his hands a lot, even on his clothes. He does that before he touches me, too. Didn't you notice"

"Guess I didn't pay attention." Nat shifted in her chair. "Sounds like it worries you. Maybe he's just a clean freak."

"That does worry me. Remember psychology was my minor, too. We studied a lot about OCD."

"What is that again?"

"Obsessive Compulsive Disorder. Repetitive behaviors, mostly. People who have it can't relax, but need to take control of every situation, make sure they are in control. They have repetitive thoughts and behaviors that are senseless and distressing but extremely difficult to overcome. They need to check things all the time, repeatedly."

"You think Robert has that?"

"I do. Maybe. Not good." Melanie reached for her drink and wiped it off with a napkin. She laughed. "See, this is a normal thing to do when you pick up a wet glass."

"So?" Nat asked.

"So, for me it's normal to do, but for Robert he might wipe it several times making sure it was dry before putting it to his mouth. And, again before setting it down on a table."

"Can he overcome that? Is there a cure?"

"Sadly, it's chronic. People with OCD need to check things repeatedly." Mel sighed and threw off the afghan covering her legs to ward off the cold of the breeze from the Back Bay. "Yes, I think so, but I would have to do a lot of research. Too tired tonight to deal with it."

~

Natalie's thoughts spun around in her head during her drive home. She remembered the look of love Robert had given Melanie on her lanai, but looking back she also remembered some of his unusual behaviors. Melanie had lost so much with Larry's death and his indigent mother harassing her. It would be wonderful if a strong man showed love for her, but not another one with an insurmountable problem.

Maybe she should offer to take Robert in as a client at her Nat's Gym. Maybe an intensive body workout five days a week would help. That should cure him! She called Mel with her idea.

"Nat, I know you want to help, but I'm not sure

this is the right solution. Still, it wouldn't hurt to try." Melanie ended the call with Nat and pushed the button for Robert.

~

"A free gym membership? Why?" Robert sounded confused, and Mel didn't blame him. She was confused herself, about a lot of things.

"We could work out together? Nat is such a sweetheart and wanted to gift it to you. She was very impressed with you the other evening." Melanie blew a big whoosh out of her mouth as silently as possible. She hoped Robert hadn't heard. She also hoped he'd accept Nat's offer. Maybe relieving some of the stress in his life would help him settle down.

"So," she said as matter of factly as possible, "meet you there tomorrow at six?"

"You mean a.m.?"

"Yes, I can only work out for an hour because I need to rush home and get ready to teach three-year-olds. Need a lot of stamina for that," she giggled.

"Uh, can you pick me up?"

"What? You have a car." Melanie was mystified about the request.

"Not right now" he said in a low voice.

Mel could almost see him fiddling with his hands, strong ones she remembered. But, were they?

"Got towed away, repossessed."

Chapter Forty-two
Help

Melanie honked and Robert came to her car wearing some of the strangest workout attire! Maybe not too strange. Many of the men at the gym wore shirts with their favorite team names on them. But, an In-N-Out shirt? She decided to ignore it, especially after she noticed he wiped the handle of her passenger side door before getting in. He bounced in and grinned. *Please, God, guide me.*

"So, you ready for this?" She knew it was a lame question, but her mind didn't take her anywhere else. She put her little car in gear and revved it. "This will be fun, and Nat is a great trainer. She will evaluate you and guide you."

"I hope so," he said. "Is there a way to wipe off the equipment after someone else has used it, like before I do?"

"Of course. All gyms have those bottles of sanitizing stuff and towels to do that." She decided to get brave. "Why? You worried about germs?"

"Uh, sort of. Didn't always, but after Dartha's

death, the worry got to me."

"Wanna share? I'm a good listener."

"Not yet."

Mel pulled up into the parking spot, killed the motor (she chuckled using that old expression from her dad) and jumped out. "Let's go!"

~

The first ten-minute workout session was a disaster. Robert was more concerned about how clean the machines were than listening to Natalie. Finally, Nat pulled on his arm and propelled him into her office. She pulled out the comfortable chair Claire had gifted her with and pushed him into it. Thank goodness for Claire who had become a soulmate. She remembered when she had collapsed in the older woman's arms sobbing and seeking solace for her loneliness. Claire, the matchmaker who had orchestrated bringing her son Nick and Emily the Feng Shui designer together. Their wedding in Nat's Gym was definitely unique and very special. The Mother and Son dance was the highlight. Nat blinked the memories away as Robert wiped his hands on his tee shirt and pulled the chair up close to her desk making sure his knees didn't touch.

She resisted her overwhelming curiosity to ask about the famous burger restaurant's shirt. Maybe it was his favorite lunch spot. After all, its corporate headquarters were located a stone's throw away in Irvine. Then, she remembered Mel telling her about the IHOP experience. Usually the burger place's shirt was amusing attire for teens and employees. She decided to ignore the shorts, too – the long ones with palm trees on them. Obviously, Robert didn't have a clue about gym attire. He was a strange duck.

"What gives, Robert?" She leaned forward in her chair and tried to lock eyes with him. She must have succeeded. He lifted his chin, and when he looked at her face his eyes glistened and he shrugged.

"Tell me, please. This is confidential between you and me. I need to know," she went on, "why a young virile man is so reluctant to even step on a treadmill. I am a good trainer, but I want to help. I can only help if the person I am training or helping is open to my suggestions. You are not. That disturbs me."

Robert shrugged again. Natalie almost gave up. She knew about his OCD, but why was he so stubborn? Must be another reason. So, she tried another tactic.

~

Robert could hardly believe he was looking at photos of Melanie on every machine. The stair stepper, the treadmill, and even the one for exercising his inner thighs. She was so beautiful, even in black and white. He knew it was a silly exercise Natalie had concocted, but it did encourage him. Seeing the woman he loved staring at him every time he took a step was motivating. Maybe Natalie should be a therapist. She was so on point.

Natalie had another suggestion. He wasn't sure about it, but he listened.

"Melanie," she said, "needs support."

"For?" Robert questioned because he knew Melanie as a strong woman. She needed support?

"For dealing with the Francine situation, the homeless mother of Larry." She looked at Robert straight on. He nodded. Did he understand how important this was? He had the expertise to help, the empathy for Melanie. Would he step up and help?

~

Melanie dropped Robert off at his odd digs, a trailer park in the Back Bay. He noticed her eyebrows raised, in question? Why was he living in a rental? If he was truly a successful therapist he should at least own a condo, if not a house. He thought to explain, then decided it was not necessary, private. After he wiped the door handle and let himself inside he collapsed on the settee.

"Need help, Lord. Please." It was all he had in him to ask for.

Something stirred in him, made his brain come alive and excited for the first time in years, in the years since Dartha's death. Was it something Natalie said? About giving Melanie support? Could he? Did he have the training and expertise to do it?

Robert called his own therapist, actually a student therapist he had supervised over ten years ago. He had total confidence in him and knew he had trained him well. Jim Stanford never alluded to their relationship, he kept everything confidential and asked all the right questions to make Robert explore the answers on his own. It was an unusual relationship, not one the licensing board would recommend, but it worked for them, and Robert was grateful.

That afternoon he settled in the comfy chair in Jim Stanford's office. Jim was in a companion one next to his. Jim folded his hands and laughed lightly. "Let the session begin."

Robert laughed, too, and started to talk. He shared from the beginning. He remembered Melanie hesitantly walking into the grief group, how shy she was, how scared and uncertain. His heart had thumped and he immediately felt drawn to her. He stood up and took her hand to lead her to the only empty seat in the circle, the one next to him. It certainly hadn't hurt that she was beautiful with a full cascade of soft brown curly hair. But, her tentative smile warmed Robert's heart. He was smitten. When he finished he cast a glimpse toward Jim whose eyes were almost closed. Had he fallen asleep listening to Robert's boring story for over forty minutes? Robert cleared his throat, and Jim's eyes flew open. "Is that all?" he asked.

"Uh, I need to find the courage to help her, and," he hesitated, "to tell her how I feel."

"How do you feel?" Both men knew it was a redundant question, but Robert knew the drill, knew Jim wanted him to verbalize it, own it.

"I love her." It was barely a whisper.

"What did you say?"

Robert cleared his throat again. This time he spoke with conviction in a normal voice. "I said I love her."

"So, you've answered your own question, Robert. Now, what are you going to do about it?"

"Tell her?"

"Just like that? Just walk up to her and say, 'I love you, Melanie?'"

"Of course not. But, I can help her with her crazy, homeless mother-in-law."

"How?"

"Not sure, gotta figure that out."

Jim looked oddly at him and sighed. "You sure you can do all that?"

The words had nothing to do with Melanie or Francine. Or, maybe they did.

BONNIE ENGSTROM

Chapter Forty-three
Confession

Confess your sins. Wasn't there a Bible verse about that, about how God will redeem us if we confess? Was it in Psalms? Was having OCD a sin? He called Natalie. He trusted her, and she seemed like a sensible woman with no agenda to change him or push him toward Melanie, except encouraging him to exercise looking at Mel's lovely face in photos. He remembered hearing somewhere she had studied psychology in college. Hopefully, she had learned about OCD. Step number one, she agreed to meet him.

They settled at a round sort of private table in Starbucks. Robert guessed it was mostly private because all the other patrons were focused on their laptops or phones or companions. No one paid attention to him and Nat. He boldly approached the meeting with a loaded question and was so nervous he almost knocked over the coffee Nat had ordered for him. Natalie laid a hand on his arm and smiled. "Calm down, Robert. Whatever you need to say is confidential.

Okay?"

He nodded but felt his lips quiver when he smiled. Nat was such a good person. He was counting on her to help him. With extreme effort and wiping his hands as unobtrusively as he could on his lap under the edge of the table, he blurted it out.

"What do you know about sin, Natalie?"

"Whoa Robert." Nat leaned back in her chair and crossed her arms across her chest. "Where did that come from?"

"That probably wasn't the right question, Nat. So, here is the real one. I know you studied psychology in school, and I know you are a woman of faith who reads her Bible. I'm pretty sure you also know I have a problem with repetitive gestures." She nodded and laid her hand back on his arm. A warm feeling crept over him.

"This is taking a lot of courage for me to ask you, but do you think having my problem is a sin?"

Nat pulled out her cellphone and clicked. What was she doing? Ignoring his desperate question?

She turned the screen on her phone to him displaying James 5:16.

"Therefore confess your sins to each other and pray for each other so that you may be healed. The prayer of a righteous person is powerful and effective."

"Now," she said in a rather matter of fact manner, "let's figure out how to help you."

~

Robert let his hands drop to his side instead of

wiping the door handle to his apartment. "I can do this." It worked, but he felt guilty. He walked into the kitchen and pulled a meal out of the freezer. He prayed while trying to avoid wiping the dinner and the microwave handle. It worked and he pushed the button for five minutes. He was so excited that he decided to treat himself to a wine spritzer. But, how would he open the bottle?

~

"Mel, I need your help. I can't do this on my own. He's your guy, Mel." Nat put down the phone and hoped Melanie would listen to the message. If she doesn't, she may have to call in the forces, all the Candy Canes from far and wide. Why was this problem given to her? Why was she the one to help?

~

"What? He came to you?" Mel tossed her work tennies into the basket by the front door while holding her phone to her ear. She flopped on the ugly sofa, put her feet up on the coffee table and asked, "Why?"

"Pretty obvious, don't you think?"

"Okay, I'll play. He trusts you more than me. He is super confused. He's in love with me?" Oh, my, why did she say that one?

"Try numbers two and three."

"What can I do, Nat? I really care for him, and have been so grateful for his support, but," she whooshed out a huge sigh. "I'm not ready to claim my love for anyone . . . yet."

"I know. Too soon after Larry's death." Nat replied.

"That and dealing with the fact he deceived me, died before we even had a marriage in the true sense, then – ugh – left me the burden of his mother. I am the one who should be seeking psych help."

"I agree, but any ideas how to help Robert? Or, should I call the troops?"

"Mmm. Don't flip, but can you guess who comes to mind?

"I don't even have to ask. Are you sure that's fair to her?"

Chapter Forty-four
Vivian and Robert

Vivian clasped her hands and raised them above her head. "Thank you, Lord, for a new project. Thank you for the trust these girls have in me. Please fill me with wisdom."

"What the heck are you doing?" Bill sounded annoyed, but she knew he was just mystified, never liked to be in the shadows.

"I," she pointed to her heart, "am praising." She grinned widely and noticed it had an effect on him. Maybe she should do that more often.

"I am the newly appointed problem solver."

"Of?" This time he didn't seem so happy.

"Love!"

She heard him mumbling "What about me?" right before she put her arms around his receding back. She closed the bedroom door behind them.

~

"She said yes?"

"What did you think she would say?" Natalie asked. "She's been the ultimate problem solver for as long as . . ."

"But, don't she and Bill have the notable, and homeless, Francine there still? At their house?" She chastised herself for her sarcasm. She knew Nat would understand, even chuckled.

"I'm not sure, but Vivian does send updates to me periodically. They do," Nat continued, "have those two extra guest rooms. Mmm, maybe Vivian has something in mind."

"I'm sure she does, but it's my problem, not hers. Makes me feel so guilty foisting the Robert problem off on her too, and Bill."

"Okay, Mel," Natalie fired back, "what exactly is the Robert problem? Or, to be more blunt, girlfriend, what are you scared of?"

Silence.

"Hello!" Nat almost yelled in the phone. Did she hear weeping?

"Scared. You're right. Scared."

"Of?"

"My own feelings."

"Such as?" Melanie could tell Nat was getting weary of this conversation, if that's what it was.

"Not right to care for someone new after Larry. I gave my heart to him, and my vows."

"Sorry to be blunt, Mel, but Larry deceived you. Yes," she went on, "he did love you, and you loved him. But . . . now here's the blunt part. Larry is dead." Natalie obviously couldn't stop herself. "Sorry. Truth." She stopped speaking again to maybe catch her breath. "Your marriage was never consummated, right?"

"Aw, . . . no."

"But, it was legal." Nat paused and went on.

"Nothing you can do about that, except maybe the Francine burden. That part of the puzzle is up to you – take it, her, or leave it, her. No one will think less of you if you ditch her. She has become your albatross. But," Natalie pressed on, "you have a life to live."

"I feel so guilty." Sob. "I trusted Larry so much. Never occurred to me he was deceptive. What is wrong with me?"

"Nothing. Unless trusting too much counts." Mel could hear Nat sigh, in frustration? Why was she burdening her friend with this?

"This isn't your problem, Nat. I need to take ownership of it and figure it out."

"Now you're talking, girl. Do that. And, invite Robert for dinner, or at least coffee."

~

Robert almost dropped the phone. There was an old joke in that, wasn't there? He laughed to himself glad he still had a sense of humor, if only a flimsy one. He drew his attention back to Melanie's voice. Coffee? She'd baked cookies? Choc chip, his fav. Seven o'clock tonight? He grabbed a frozen meal and tossed it in the microwave before he realized he didn't wipe the container off, nor the oven handle. Was the therapy session with Jim working?

He ate quickly, almost gobbling his orange chicken and hoping it wouldn't lie like a boulder in his stomach. It would be so embarrassing to belch in front of Melanie. But, he remembered she worked with little kids, so she probably heard a lot of belching every day. Just not from adults.

He called Jim but got his voicemail. Not wanting to make a big deal of it, he hung up without leaving a message. He didn't want to seem like a sad case to the younger man.

How was he going to get to Melanie's? He had no car since he'd neglected to pay his bills and messed up his funds. Newport Beach didn't have a real bus service, only the county one that ran between it and Santa Ana and Costa Mesa, used mostly by day workers. There was the beach one the surfers and Orange County College students took, but it had very specific routes. Did he have enough cash for a cab or a Lyft? He felt his pockets – just a few coins. He knew he had money in his bank account, and a debit card, but he didn't trust using the plastic thing. He'd have to wipe it off before and after handing it to a driver. What had his life come to? A woman he barely knew driving him and asking him to after dinner coffee at her house. At least he had been able to walk to Jim Stanford's office, and Jim had graciously driven him home to his tiny rented trailer in the Back Bay. Something had to give in his life, soon.

His phone chimed again. He wasn't sure if it was his cellphone or the landline, so he quickly wiped off both with a handy baby wipe. After feeling vibration in his pocket and pulling it out again he realized it was the cell. Melanie. Was she cancelling?

"Hi, friend. I forgot you have no transportation. Pick you up in ten minutes?"

He waited at the entrance to the trailer park so she wouldn't have to see his dilapidated abode. He prayed, hard, hoping he could manage to open her car door and get in without wiping the handle and the seat. He had done it before when she drove him after the grief group, but everything had happened so fast he hadn't had time.

Time. Maybe that's what he needed to deal with. If he could eliminate time, giving him no time to worry or wipe, maybe he could be cured.

Mel pulled up, rolled down the passenger window and waved. Her smile was so wonderful. There was no other word for it. If a smile could fill a heart, hers did the trick. Without a thought he jumped in. Mel grinned and his world lit up. Then he started to sweat.

He had forgotten. No wiping. Was Melanie his earthly savior?

~

"You all right?" Mel glanced him a curious look. "Is it too hot in here? I can turn up the AC."

"No, fine. Just rushing. Looking forward to those yummy cookies."

"I think they're still warm. Coffee is brewing. Looking forward to a chat."

A chat. Melanie expected a chat. About him? Or, her problems with Francine? Or him and her? Was he up to this?

He managed to get out of the car and follow her into her apartment without making a scene wiping. He had held himself together. Because of Melanie? Maybe she is his earthly savior. What would Jim think?

They settled at her counter bar area munching cookies and sipping very dark coffee in a cup she had just taken from the dishwasher. He poured more creamer in his and she laughed.

"A throwback to my semester in France in grad school. Loved the café au lait idea." He laughed back.

"Didn't know that about you, Robert. How fun. Is that where you met your wife?"

"Yes, met Dartha there sitting in a café. Never

looked back." He shifted in his chair.

"So, Melanie, why am I here? You must have something up your sleeve." Robert gritted his teeth. He didn't usually make such a bold statement. Why was he here?

"I don't mean to sound ungrateful," he paused and gulped. "But we hardly know each other, even though," he paused again, "I'd like to know you better. Much better," he added. How had he gotten so brave?

Melanie reached her hand across the counter and grasped his. His trembled and he pulled it away. He couldn't, just couldn't, wipe his when she was demonstrating her friendship. He put his hand in his pocket, felt for a wipe peeking out of the container and ran his fingers on it.

"Robert, I am going to be bold. I need your advice."

That's it, advice? Not friendship or love?

"You know about Francine because I've shared it in grief group." Mel lowered her head and wrung her hands together. "I don't know what to do about her. I don't know what's right." She raised her face and looked Robert in the eyes. "I know you are a man of faith, a kind man who relies on the Lord for direction and wisdom. What should I do about Francine?"

~

Robert flopped on his bed, rather unceremoniously without wiping the pillow or sheets, not even wiping the door handle when he returned home. No, he mustn't think about anything, just chill.

But, he couldn't avoid Melanie's questions, nor her genuine concerns. She was in a tough spot. Who would ever have guessed dead Larry's estranged mother would show up and impede Melanie's life? The woman was an anomaly. She seemed to have come out of nowhere. Robert wondered if she was from the devil, or if God wanted Melanie to rescue her. Not his call, but he clasped his hands and prayed for Mel for wisdom, and courage. Would the God he drifted away from after Dartha's death help the woman he loved now?

BONNIE ENGSTROM

Chapter Forty-five
Melanie

"I am ready to face my ghosts," Melanie shrieked into the mirror. The glass didn't respond, and her visage didn't change. Still, she felt stronger inside than she had for months. The mirror was a good listener, the kind she liked by not arguing with her or correcting her or, especially not, questioning her. She knew she could call her Candy Cane sisters, knew they would pray for her, knew they wouldn't argue or try to change her mind. But, this decision was hers alone, hers and God's. She squared her shoulders, clasped her hands in front of her chest and grinned. "I am strong!"

The first thing she did was gather all the photos and memorabilia from her romance with Larry. She stuffed them into a flower-printed box she'd been keeping to give a gift in. No matter, this was a gift to herself. Since she had printed out all the numerous wedding photos the photographer and others had taken, she deleted them all from her phone. She handprinted a big label and stuck it on the side of the box – My life and love with Larry. Just in case there ever would be progeny in her future she dated it. If she was ever blessed to have grandchildren, they should have knowledge about that agonizing period in her life. She kissed the top of the box and lifted the heavy lid of the ancient Cedar chest her Pap-Pap had made for her Nan-Nan almost a century ago. Why she'd kept it she wasn't sure. Perhaps because she had so few things from them. Maybe Susan her mother had more. She would ask later.

When Natalie answered sounding tired after a long day at her gym, Melanie practically shouted, "I am ready to face my ghosts!"

"Praise God, Mel. Tell me. You just gave me the inspiration I need. Tired tonight, but this did the trick. Tell all."

It only took fifteen minutes, and Melanie was ready to roll. Next, she called her mother. Susan was ecstatic. "I've been praying so hard for this moment. Now what?"

They sent cyber hugs through the phone, and Melanie pressed on to make another call.

"Robert, I need to talk with you." Unfortunately, she had to leave a message hoping he would listen.

"Vivian, need to talk with you. You there?"

"Here, girl. Just finishing up a salad. What's up?" The older woman sounded breathless. Was she okay? Was Bill being a pill?

"Vivian, I am ready to face my ghosts"

"Oh, my. Prayers answered. Explain."

Melanie shared every detail with Vivian, as every Candy Cane always did. She was their ultimate mother, she understood all. Finally, Vivian spoke. Her voice was strong and calm.

"I am so glad, so happy for you, Melanie. Please be assured of that. But, you still have one decision to make."

"Francine?"

"Yes."

"She still there at your house?"

"Yes. But some things have changed."

~

Melanie parked her little car in the expansive driveway of the Lord's Newport Coast house. She pranced up the flagstone walk and didn't even bother to ring the bell. She was family.

The woman who answered the door was not Vivian. She hardly recognized Francine in a sort of maid's uniform. Just a blue dress and an apron tied at her waist. Not homeless clothes.

"What's with the get-up?" Mel asked before the other woman could say the obligatory, "Welcome to the Lord's house."

Francine's hands fluttered like hummingbirds searching for nectar. She reached for Mel's hands, then pulled away when Mel didn't respond. "It's me, really me," she said.

"What happened?" She couldn't help asking. "Why?"

"Long story. You wanna come in and listen?" She grasped at Mel's hands again and pulled her toward the sofa.

She lifted the cross hanging from her throat. "This is what happened."

BONNIE ENGSTROM

Chapter Forty-six
Closure

Relief! Blessed relief.

Melanie tugged the afghan on the sofa up to her neck. Closing her eyes, she sighed. Was it all really over? Could she lead a normal life again? With no ghosts?

Learning that Francine was safe and secure and no longer homeless made her heart pound. Vivian had worked her magic, her godly magic. Francine was part of the Bill and Vivian Lord's household now, and thankfully Bill Lord loved having her there. No waiting for Viv to make coffee in the morning or fix his peanut butter toast snack in afternoon. She never did learn why Francine abandoned her toddler son, nor about Francine's claim to having cancer. Another hoax? Or, had God healed her with the treatments she hated? According to Vivian the silver fish forks suddenly reappeared in the drawer of the sideboard all polished brightly. And the missing broach turned up in a bathroom drawer. "Maybe I misplaced it," Vivian said.

Although Bill didn't say so, Melanie was sure the

"good dentist friend" he referred to was part of the secret philanthropy group. She also wondered if the friend might be her own dentist, about Bill's age, handsome and obviously wealthy. Why wealthy she wasn't sure. Something he had said once about owning an island; also, the way he conducted himself and the ring on his pinky and the car in the Fashion Island parking lot next to the medical building, the license plate declaring DRSMILE. He wasn't a pretentious man, but self-assured and kind. If whomever Bill's friend was, she was sure Francine would have a beautiful smile in a few months.

She did learn about Carlos. Just a smidgeon. Neither he nor Francine knew about the origin of the package she received. It was anonymously sent to Carlos' postal box via U.S. Postal Service, no return address. It contained photos of Larry as a little boy and as a groom at his wedding. Mel had no recollection of sending any, certainly not from the wedding, and she'd had no access to childhood photos. Who had sent them? All Mel could think about was Larry from heaven. Was that possible? Had anyone thought to look at the postal date on the package?

Then she thought about Robert.

She knew she wasn't ready for a relationship, especially not a love relationship. As much as she vacillated between loving Larry and despising him for his deception, the pendulum swung toward love. She couldn't just bury love, stuff it in a bag and toss it. Love was a huge part of her being now. She still needed to feel it and embrace it. They had come so close in so many ways, just not physically. She was grateful for that. It meant she would have no haunting memories or dreams about consummating their love. Well, dreams maybe, but she had no control over those. So, here she was a thirty-two-year old virgin. Oops, with an abortion behind her. Hopefully God understood because society, if it knew, would censure her.

Courage. She pressed the green button and heard his voice. How could she explain? He had been her anchor.

"I know why you're calling, Melanie." His voice was steady with only a slight catch in it. "I understand."

"Oh, Robert, I am so sorry to be such a ditz." She sobbed hoping he wouldn't hear her anguish.

"It's really okay, Mel. I do understand. And," he paused dramatically, "I want to thank you for your help."

"My help?" she gulped. "How?"

"Because of you I am on the road to recovery. Not one hundred percent yet but walking that road with confidence.

"You must never blame yourself for anything that happened with Larry, nor between us. It was all ordained by God."

"You think so?"

"I know so." His voice stopped, and Melanie wondered if he was still there. She heard a hiccup and some wiping. Of the phone?

"Please, Melanie, know that because of your friendship and acceptance of me the way I am, you made a difference. I am on the path to healing. Now, it's time to say goodnight."

BONNIE ENGSTROM

Epilogue

Melanie pulled on the silly tennies she wore to teach three-year-olds who spilled juice and jelly. She noticed a purple stain on the left one. Tonight - in the wash for sure. With bleach.

She hummed the ancient tune *Jesus Loves Me*, the one she'd taught her tiny students, the one they sang at the Spring Pageant. They were always so adorable waving to their parents and sometimes stepping out of line, mostly because they had to go potty. Melanie or her co-teacher Nora grabbed a little hand and trekked back to the small restroom. Sometimes Miss Dana beat them to it so they could stay with their charges.

Today would be a good day, one of those God shared in Ecclesiastes 7:14.

When times are good, be happy; but when times are bad, consider this: God has made the one as well as the other. Therefore, no one can discover anything about their future.

God was in her corner. Francine was taken care of, possibly even betrothed to the delivery guy Carlos. Larry was buried. She had ordered a tombstone so she could visit when in Arizona. Robert was going to be okay working on his OCD problems with his psychologist friend who was now mentoring him. A reversal of order.

Melanie smiled at her students and settled them in their seats. "Let's start the day with one of our favorite songs. Who remembers Jesus Loves Me?"

Little Jackson, the student she'd had the most trouble with, raised his tiny hand. "Does it start like this, Miss Melanie?"

THE END

This book is a sequel to Melanie's Blue Skirt.
What will become of the skirt now?
And the blue diamond ring?

About Bonnie

This is the seventh book in the Candy Cane Girls series. All are set in Newport Beach, California, with a few scenes set in Scottsdale, Arizona, both places Bonnie calls home.

She and her husband, Dave, have four grandchildren in Arizona a few miles from them. Three are girls, one of which is a twin with a boy who constantly endures teasing and giggling. Fortunately, Grandpa Dave spends special guy time with him to relieve him of girly talk and share Chick-fil-A.

The other two boys live in Costa Rica - Pura Vida! - with their father who has taught them to surf, skateboard and fish for their dinners. All six children, even though separated by continents, are very close and get together at least twice a year in either Costa Rica or Arizona where the two beach boys have to wear shoes!

Bonnie and Dave believe family is all. They feel very blessed to have grandchildren nearby, even though it often interrupts their schedule.

Bonnie is a long time member of American

Christian Fiction Writers and a member of Christian Writers of the West in Arizona. She is a Pro Member of Romance Writers of America. She began her fiction writing career in California as a member of The Orange County Christian Writers Fellowship. She wrote the weekly education columns for two newspapers, The Newport Ensign and the Costa Mesa News. These organizations and the hundreds of newsletters she produced as a five time PTA president helped to hone her writing skills. The impetus for her writing was when she was the editor of her high school newspaper and wrote a weekly column for a local community paper, The Penn Hills Progress, too many years ago to mention. (Hint: She was only seventeen.)

She loves to connect with her readers. Her email address is bengstrom@hotmail.com. Be sure to put BOOK in the subject line. She would love to chat with you and answer any questions.

Visit her website http://www.bonnieengstrom.com (where you can see all those grandchildren) and link up with her on Facebook at https://www.facebook.com/bonnieengstromauthor/. To see all of her books go to http://bit.ly/2NgOiyd.

*Be sure to sign up for her next newsletter in which there will be a drawing you can win to be a character in her next book. You can sign up on her Facebook page or her website.